LIGHT AND DARK

Whoever those men were, Fargo knew they were up to no good. He leveled the Colt and shouted, "Hold it!"

"It's Fargo! Kill him!"

That removed any lingering doubts. Fargo reared back the hammer and fired. Smoke and flame geysered from the barrel of the Colt.

Fargo dove to the side as a slug sizzled past his ear. He rolled over, and came up in a crouch as he saw another pair of muzzle flashes and more lead fanged at him. He aimed at one of the flashes and squeezed the trigger, and a hoarse yell of pain rewarded him.

His satisfaction was fleeting, however. In the next instant, what felt like the side of a mountain reared up and slammed him on the side of the head. He went over backward, skyrockets exploding in his brain. That brilliant display lasted only a second before it was swept away by utter blackness. . . .

THE

TRAILSMAN

#290

MOUNTAIN
MAVERICKS

by

Jon Sharpe

A SIGNET BOOK

SIGNET
Published by New American Library, a division of
Penguin Group (USA) Inc., 375 Hudson Street,
New York, New York 10014, USA
Penguin Group (Canada), 90 Eglinton Avenue East, Suite 700, Toronto,
Ontario M4P 2Y3, Canada (a division of Pearson Penguin Canada Inc.)
Penguin Books Ltd., 80 Strand, London WC2R 0RL, England
Penguin Ireland, 25 St. Stephen's Green, Dublin 2,
Ireland (a division of Penguin Books Ltd.)
Penguin Group (Australia), 250 Camberwell Road, Camberwell, Victoria 3124,
Australia (a division of Pearson Australia Group Pty. Ltd.)
Penguin Books India Pvt. Ltd., 11 Community Centre, Panchsheel Park,
New Delhi - 110 017, India
Penguin Group (NZ), cnr Airborne and Rosedale Roads, Albany,
Auckland 1310, New Zealand (a division of Pearson New Zealand Ltd.)
Penguin Books (South Africa) (Pty.) Ltd., 24 Sturdee Avenue,
Rosebank, Johannesburg 2196, South Africa

Penguin Books Ltd., Registered Offices:
80 Strand, London WC2R 0RL, England

First published by Signet, an imprint of New American Library,
a division of Penguin Group (USA) Inc.

First Printing, December 2005
10 9 8 7 6 5 4 3 2 1

The first chapter of this book previously appeared in *Renegade Raiders*, the
two hundred eighty-ninth volume in this series.

Copyright © Penguin Group (USA) Inc., 2005
All rights reserved

 REGISTERED TRADEMARK—MARCA REGISTRADA

The Trailsman

Beginnings . . . they bend the tree and they mark the man. Skye Fargo was born when he was eighteen. Terror was his midwife, vengeance his first cry. Killing spawned Skye Fargo, ruthless, cold-blooded murder. Out of the acrid smoke of gunpowder still hanging in the air, he rose, cried out a promise never forgotten.

The Trailsman they began to call him all across the West: searcher, scout, hunter, the man who could see where others only looked, his skills for hire but not his soul, the man who lived each day to the fullest, yet trailed each tomorrow. Skye Fargo, the Trailsman, the seeker who could take the wildness of a land and the wanting of a woman and make them his own.

The Montana high country, 1860—
where the most dangerous beasts
go on two legs instead of four.

1

The young woman burst out into the clearing, running hard. Her dark braids trailed out behind her head, and her breasts heaved under her buckskin dress.

The big man, who was also dressed in buckskins, was ready for her. He stepped from behind a tree, thrust out an arm, and caught her around the waist. The impact as he pulled her to a halt staggered him a step, despite the strength in his muscular body.

She didn't gasp or scream. She just fought in silence, flailing at him with small, hard fists as she tried desperately to squirm out of his grip. But he was too strong for her. He got both arms around her, picked her up, and swung her around so that her back was pressed against the tree behind which he had hid.

Skye Fargo's lake blue eyes peered intently into the young woman's dark brown ones. He loosened his grip with one hand, lifted it, and held his forefinger to his lips in the universal sign for quiet.

He stood close to her so that her breasts touched his chest. Fargo was aware of that contact and under other circumstances would have found it quite pleasurable.

Right now, however, he had other things on his mind—like the crashing sounds in the brush that allowed him to track the progress of the young woman's pursuers as they came closer.

She had stopped trying to fight him and was staring at him in confusion instead. Fargo wasn't sure yet what tribe she was from, so he used sign language to tell her that he was a friend. She relaxed slightly, but he could tell that her body was still poised for flight.

Fargo dropped his right hand to the walnut grips of the Colt revolver holstered on his hip. He eased her farther around the tree with his left hand and stepped back, hoping that she wouldn't run.

She didn't. She stayed where she was, her back against the tree, and watched him. Every few seconds her eyes cut nervously toward the sounds of the approaching riders.

"Damn it, I know good and well she came this way. I saw her run into the woods."

It was a man's voice, rough and husky, about twenty yards away. A second man asked, "You sure you didn't just imagine it because you been so long without a woman, Devlin?"

"No, blast it. I saw her! If you think I'm lyin', you can go to hell!"

"Take it easy. If she's in here, we'll find her."

They would find more than they bargained for, thought Fargo.

The hour was late afternoon. He had made camp in a clearing not far from the Yellowstone River. The thickly wooded slopes of Crazy Peak rose a short distance to the north. A narrow, fast-flowing creek ran through the woods only a short distance from the clearing before merging with the Yellowstone. Fargo had hooked a couple of nice trout in the creek and had been about to start cleaning them for his supper with the Arkansas toothpick when he'd heard someone running through the trees toward his camp.

Fargo hadn't lived as long as he had on the frontier without learning a few things—such as how to be careful. He had warned the big black-and-white Ovaro stallion to be quiet. Then he stepped behind the tree to see what was going to happen.

He didn't know what to expect. His mind was open. But he had been a little surprised anyway when he saw the young, pretty Indian woman run into his camp.

Now the voices he heard explained a great deal by their mere presence. It was a couple of white men chasing an Indian girl through the woods. . . . They could have only one thing in mind.

All across the frontier, a decent woman was sacrosanct. Not even the most bloody-handed reiver would molest a woman.

But for most men that only applied to white women. Indian squaws were different, fair game for a man who hadn't been with a gal for a while.

Anger burned in Fargo's belly. He didn't believe in taking a woman—any woman—by force. A man who would do that was lower than a snake and deserved whatever he got. He found himself almost hoping that the two riders in the woods would find the camp.

But it would be better for the young woman behind him if they didn't. You never knew what might happen in a fight. Random violence was no respecter of persons. If it came down to shooting, she might be hit by a stray bullet. Fargo was reasonably confident he could handle any threat the two men represented, but it was impossible to guarantee that.

So he hoped they would just ride on without discovering him and the young woman. It was possible.

He hadn't started a fire yet, so they wouldn't smell any smoke. And the woods were thick. The men might pass within fifty feet of the camp and never see it.

Fargo glanced over at the stallion. The Ovaro's head was up, his ears cocked. He knew there were other horses around, and his instinct was to call out to them. But Fargo had asked for quiet, and the stallion was well-trained enough to follow that command, even though it was hard.

The other horses suddenly nickered. They had scented the Ovaro. Fargo's jaw tightened under his close-cropped dark beard. The reaction of their mounts was liable to make the men more suspicious.

Sure enough, one of them said, "The horses are actin' like there's something over there."

"Let's take a look."

The hoofbeats and the crackling of brush came even closer. The men were almost on top of the camp.

Fargo held his left hand out toward the young woman, motioning for her to stay where she was. He moved farther out into the clearing, so that he would be clearly visible to the two men. He wanted their attention focused on him.

They reined in sharply as they rode out of the woods and saw the broad-shouldered man in buckskins and a brown hat waiting for them. Fargo stood there casually, his left hand at his belt, his right hanging beside the butt of the Colt.

"Howdy, boys," he said.

There were only two of them, for which Fargo was grateful. Though he had heard only two voices, it had been possible that there were more men who had simply remained silent.

To start with, the one on Fargo's right was burly and made even more so by the thick, buffalo-hide coat he wore. He had a short brown beard on a pugnacious jaw. A battered old hat with a round crown and a narrow brim was pushed down over a thatch of tangled brown hair. He glared at Fargo.

The second man was slender and clean shaven, with sandy hair down to his shoulders. He wore a cowhide vest over a gray wool shirt, and had a black hat cocked back on his head. His expression was more surprised than angry.

Both men were heavily armed, wearing holstered revolvers and sheathed knives. Rifle butts stuck up from saddle scabbards. Clearly, they were tough hombres.

But there were only two of them, Fargo reminded himself, and neither of them had a gun drawn.

"Who the hell are you?" the one in the buffalo coat demanded.

Normally, Fargo would have been a little offended at being addressed in such an arrogant tone. Now he just kept a faint smile on his face as he said, "Just a fella who's camping here for the night."

The smaller man drawled, "Did you see a squaw come runnin' through here a few minutes ago?"

The tree behind which the young woman hid had a thick trunk. The men couldn't see her from where they were. Fargo didn't even glance in her direction as he said, "You boys are the first folks I've seen all day."

That wasn't true, of course, and Fargo didn't like to lie. He thought this one was justified, though. He might still be able to turn the pursuers away without a fight. That would be the safest in the long run for the woman.

"You hear anything, maybe somebody runnin' through the woods?"

Fargo shook his head and said, "Nope. Just your horses. That's all I heard."

The one in the buffalo coat sniffed, drawing in a big breath of air. He glowered at Fargo and said to his companion, "He's lyin'. I can *smell* that Injun gal."

The second man smiled thinly. "Well, now," he said without taking his eyes off Fargo, "if there's one thing Devlin here knows how to do, it's sniff out Injuns. You want to reconsider your answer, amigo?"

Fargo shook his head. "Nope."

"He's hidin' her!" the burly man accused. "He wants her for hisself! I say we kill him and then hunt that bitch down!" His hand moved toward the butt of the gun at his waist.

The other man put out a hand to stop him. "Take it easy, Devlin," he ordered in a tone of easy command. To Fargo, he said, "Look, be reasonable, amigo. A squaw ain't worth dyin' over. Just tell us which way she went, and we'll let you live." An ugly grin quirked his mouth. "Hell, you help us find her, and we might even share her with you."

"You better turn and ride away while you still can," Fargo said.

The grin disappeared from the man's face. "If that's the way you want it—"

His hand stabbed toward his gun.

Fargo figured that the slender man was the faster of the two. That meant he had to be dealt with first. With blinding speed, Fargo palmed out his Colt and fired from the hip.

Even as fast as Fargo was, the man managed to get his gun out and squeeze off a shot. The two blasts blended into one. Fargo's bullet was a hair swifter, however, fast enough to throw off the man's aim as it slammed into his shoulder and slewed him sideways in the saddle. His lead gouged into the ground just to the right of Fargo's booted feet.

Another gun roared, hard on the heels of the first

two shots. The burly man was slower on the draw, all right, but still plenty fast enough to be dangerous. Fargo felt as much as heard the wind-rip of the bullet beside his ear as he pivoted smoothly toward his second antagonist and fired again.

He had hoped to wound Devlin as he had the other man. But just as Fargo pulled the trigger, Devlin's horse spooked at the gunfire and jerked to one side. The slug from Fargo's gun drove deeply into Devlin's chest instead of shattering his shoulder. Devlin rocked back in the saddle, his eyes going wide with pain and shock.

Devlin's gun hand drooped. He struggled mightily to bring it up again, but he was too weak. He swayed from side to side. His thumb looped over the revolver's hammer and slowly pulled it back.

Then, as he hunched over from a fresh burst of agony, his finger clenched on the trigger and fired the gun again. The bullet hammered into the ground beside his horse. The animal reared up in fear and threw Devlin off. The man landed on the ground with a heavy thud and didn't move again.

It had taken only a handful of heartbeats. Fargo turned toward the other man again, but he was gone. A rataplan of hoofbeats echoing through the trees told Fargo that the man was fleeing. He had been hit hard, hard enough so that he was out of the fight. Now he was just trying to save his life.

A grim expression was etched onto Fargo's face as he stalked across the clearing and checked the man in the buffalo coat. Devlin was dead, staring up sightlessly at the canopy of pine branches above him. Even in the fading light, Fargo could see that life had departed from the man's piggish eyes.

He swung around sharply and holstered the Colt. As he did so, the young woman stepped out from behind the tree where she had been hiding. She paused, trembling a little like a deer about to bolt. Fargo knew she was thinking about running again, running away from him this time.

But he didn't know if Devlin and the other man had had any friends with them. The woman might be safer staying with him, at least for a while.

"Take it easy," Fargo said, knowing she probably didn't speak English, but hoping the calm sound of his voice would steady her nerves. "We'll get out of here, just in case that son of a bitch tries to double back on us."

"Son of a bitch," the Indian woman repeated.

Fargo had to smile. She knew what he meant by that, anyway. He nodded as he picked up his saddle blanket and tossed it on the Ovaro's back.

It took only a few minutes for Fargo to get the stallion saddled and ready to ride. The woman stood there watching him. He picked up the two fish he had caught and looped the stringer they were attached to around the saddle horn. That was all the packing he had to do. He swung up onto the Ovaro and walked the horse across the clearing. When he reached the young woman, he held out a hand to her.

She hesitated only a second, then grasped his hand. They locked wrists, and Fargo pulled her up easily behind him. She straddled the Ovaro and slipped her arms around Fargo's waist to hang on.

He rode out of the trees, following the creek down to the river about a quarter of a mile away, and then turned west along the Yellowstone, heeling the stallion into a ground-eating trot.

Springtime in the high country was a changeable season. Though the days were warm and the grass had started to green up and bright bits of colorful wildflowers poked through here and there from the ground, the nights were still cold. There was always a chance that a late-season blizzard might come rolling down out of Canada and blanket the countryside with a thick layer of snow.

Fargo thought that in many ways this was the prettiest time of year in the mountains, and he was glad to be here. He had no particular destination. After wintering at a trading post back in Nebraska Territory, he had gotten the urge to see the Pacific Ocean again. But the Pacific coast stretched for a long way, so wherever he wound up was fine. He had won enough money playing poker during the long, cold winter months so he was able to outfit himself for the trip. Game was plentiful; he would hunt his food most of the way.

Being fiddle-footed was its own peculiar blessing and curse at the same time. Fargo rode wherever the frontier trails took him, worked only when it was necessary or when he wanted to, and surrounded himself with the splendors of a vast, untamed land. But he was human, too, and the fact that he had never put down roots sometimes bothered him. Not enough so to make him change his way of living, but enough that he was aware of it.

Today, though, he had simply been happy to ride through this rugged, beautiful landscape, alone except for the Ovaro, feeling content with his lot in life. He had been looking forward to a supper of pan-fried trout and a good night's sleep.

Then the Indian woman had come running into his camp, followed by the pair of no-good hardcases, and once again Fargo had been reminded of how quickly and easily trouble could crop up on the frontier.

The sun had set behind the mountains to the west. Darkness fell quickly. Fargo kept the Ovaro moving, wanting to put some distance between them and the site of the shoot-out.

He had left Devlin lying back there in the clearing. While it bothered Fargo to abandon a man's body to scavengers, there hadn't been time to dig a grave. The other man might have come back with others, bent on revenge.

Some folks called Skye Fargo the "Trailsman," because he could follow just about any trail, no matter how faint. But he also knew how to *avoid* leaving a trail, and he brought all of that skill into play as he rode west with the Indian woman.

She hung on and leaned against him in weariness. Her head rested against his shoulder. It was true that she did smell a little like bear grease, but Fargo was used to that and didn't find it offensive. Her body was warm and lush against his back, the heat of contact traveling through their buckskins.

He didn't bother asking her any questions. She seemed willing to accompany him wherever he wanted to go. For now, that meant making sure no one was on their trail. Once he was certain of that, he could try to find out where she had come from and return her to her home.

Fargo kept moving long into the night, stopping finally where the steep overhang of a bluff formed a small, cavelike area at its base. He reined in and dismounted. The woman slipped easily and lithely off the Ovaro without waiting for Fargo to help her get down.

Fargo watched, impressed, as she knelt and quickly scooped out a small depression in the sandy ground at the base of the bluff. She surrounded it with rocks and then straightened up. As she began gathering twigs and small branches from the ground under the pines that grew almost all the way up to the bluff, she pointed at the fish hanging from the saddle. Fargo grinned, slipped the Arkansas toothpick from the fringed sheath strapped to his calf, and started using the razor-sharp blade to clean the trout.

They made a good team. In what seemed like no time at all, the woman had a small fire going. Fargo started frying the fish in the pan he kept in his saddle-bags. The overhang of the bluff broke up the smoke so that it wouldn't be seen rising into the night sky. The pit the woman had dug shielded the fire itself from view.

When the food was done, they both ate hungrily. Fargo enjoyed the enthusiasm with which the woman tore off hunks of the fish and put them in her mouth. He had never cared that much for dainty women. He preferred a gal with honest appetites she knew how to satisfy.

He didn't have any other such appetites in mind for tonight, however. He hadn't rescued this woman from Devlin and the other man only to try to force his own attentions on her. He kept his distance, not wanting to spook her.

When she was finished eating, the woman leaned back against the bluff and sighed. Her face looked sleepy in the faint light from the glowing embers of the fire. Fargo stood up, went to the Ovaro, and unfastened the bedroll that was lashed to the saddle. He brought it back to the bluff and spread it out on the ground. Then he motioned for the woman to take it.

She frowned up at him, evidently not understanding. "You take the blankets and get some sleep," he told her. "I reckon you don't understand what I'm saying, do you?"

He spoke at least a smattering of most Indian languages. He tried several, telling her in each of them that she could use the bedroll. She just looked baffled. He began to wonder if she was from some tribe he had never encountered before. That was unlikely, but he supposed it was possible.

Since he didn't seem to be getting anywhere, he resorted to sign language again. He pointed to her and then to the bedroll, then placed his palms together and leaned his head against them as if he were sleeping. She smiled at him.

"Well, I reckon that's a little progress," he said. He motioned again for her to stretch out and get some rest. Instead, she pointed at him.

He jerked a thumb toward a nearby pine and said, "I'll sleep sitting up against that tree. Don't worry about me. I'll be fine."

She reached over, patted the bedroll, and pointed to him. Fargo shook his head.

The woman sighed in exasperation, got to her feet, grasped the hem of her buckskin dress, and peeled it up and over her head. She tossed the garment aside and stood nude except for her moccasins in front of Fargo.

She was lovely, no doubt about that. Her midnight black hair was parted in the middle and pulled back into two long braids that hung down her back. She had dark, intelligent eyes and strong, high-cheekboned features. Her wide shoulders helped support the firm, round breasts that rode high and proud on her chest, topped by large, dark brown nipples. Her stomach was flat and her hips were wide, flowing smoothly into muscular thighs and calves. Coppery skin was burnished by the firelight into an even deeper, richer shade of red.

She moved a step closer to Fargo and raised her hands to rest them lightly on his chest. Though she was tall for an Indian woman, she still had to tilt her head back a little to look up into his eyes. Underlying the smell of bear grease was a healthy, undeniable woman scent. Fargo felt himself getting aroused.

"Look," he said, his voice a growl, "you don't have to do this. You don't owe me a damned thing."

She leaned closer, came up on her toes, and kissed him.

Well, hell, thought Fargo as he feasted on the hot wet sweetness of her mouth, only a fool would keep arguing in a situation like this. And his mama hadn't raised any fools. . . .

He put his arms around her waist and pulled her tightly against him. One hand slipped down to caress the full roundness of her bottom. She moaned passionately as her lips parted in invitation and his tongue darted between them to explore her mouth. She brought a hand to his groin and rubbed the hardening shaft through his buckskins.

Fargo kissed and hugged and fondled her for long minutes. He cupped one of her breasts, lifting the heavy globe and thumbing the hard nipple. She tugged at his belt and the buttons of his buckskin trousers until she could slide her hands inside the garment and fill her palms with the hard, heated length of his manhood. It took both of her hands to cover his erect member. She squeezed hard on it for a moment before she broke the kiss and went to her knees in front of him. She took him in her mouth, swallowing as much as she could of the pole that jutted proudly from his groin.

Fargo closed his eyes and surrendered momentarily to the pleasure she was giving him. She sucked and stroked and licked, and each caress sent a new jolt of arousal throbbing through him. Fargo could easily have lost control and spent his seed in her mouth, but with an iron will, he reined in the urge. He wanted to give her as much as she was giving him.

She lay back on the bedroll and spread her legs wide. The triangle of thick black hair pointed like an arrow at the wet opening of her sex. Fargo finished the job of stripping off his clothes and knelt between her wide-flung thighs. His fingers went to her core, spreading the fleshy folds, and stroking her. She sighed and shuddered as his thumb toyed with the sensitive nubbin at the top of her opening. She was drenched, and her juices soon coated his hand as he played with her. Her hips pumped up and down restlessly, urgently.

Without words, her dark eyes appealed to him to take her. He moved closer and brought the head of his shaft to the proper spot. The heat of her almost made him lose control again. With a surge of his hips, he drove into her, sheathing himself deep within her heated core.

The woman cried out and threw her arms around him as he leaned over her. She held him with a desperate strength. Her knees lifted and her ankles locked together above Fargo's hips. He thrust in and out of her with a strong, regular rhythm. The woman gasped breathlessly as her excitement grew.

Like a long, glorious gallop over hills and valleys, Fargo rode her with every bit of expertise he could muster, lifting her higher and higher toward the peak of culmination. She met him thrust for thrust, her hips bouncing up off the bedroll. Fargo felt the strength in her, the smooth play of muscles, the fervor with which she gripped him. His own climax was inching closer and closer, despite his efforts to postpone it. They were both too aroused to tolerate much of a delay now.

She cried out and clutched at him and began to shake and spasm beneath him, and he knew she had tipped over the edge. With that, he let himself go, too, and surged deep inside her one final time. Holding himself there, he flooded her with his seed, emptying himself in a long, shuddering explosion of passion. He groaned as his climax swept over him.

Still locked together, they slid down the far side of the peak, breathless, their bodies covered with a fine sheen of sweat despite the coolness of the night. But as they lay there holding each other, Fargo gradually grew aware of how chilly it was getting, so he grasped one of the blankets that made up the bedroll and pulled it over them. He rolled onto his side and the woman snuggled against him. He slipped an arm around her shoulders and cuddled her against his broad, hairy chest.

She sighed in satisfaction. With both of them sated and tired, Fargo knew they might go to sleep this way. That would be all right, he thought. His Colt was in easy reach by the bedroll. The Ovaro was grazing nearby and wouldn't stray far. The big stallion was the best sentry a man could ask for. If anybody or anything came around that represented a threat, the horse would let Fargo know right away. He wasn't worried about dozing off.

As weary as they both were, though, the woman evidently wasn't through. She slid a hand down Fargo's belly under the blanket and found his shaft, which was now growing soft again after his climax. She wrapped her fingers around it, and her touch wakened new life within the thick member. She stroked it slowly, lazily, evidently content just to caress him for now.

Fargo turned his head and planted a kiss on the top of her head as she nestled against his shoulder. "You're a mighty sweet gal," he murmured. "Too bad we don't speak the same lingo. I'd sure like to know your name."

"It's Elizabeth," she said as she squeezed his shaft. "Elizabeth McAllister."

2

Fargo jerked upright, throwing off the blanket. He wasn't an easily surprised man, but the perfect English with which she had just answered him came as a complete shock.

She didn't seem startled by his reaction. She was lying there shaking with laughter. "Oh, my," she said. "You should see your face. . . . Now you have the advantage over me. I was going to call you by name, but I don't know it."

"Skye Fargo," he bit off.

"Skye . . . an unusual name, but it suits you." Elizabeth McAllister sat up and grew more serious. "I'm sorry, Skye. I know it was mean of me to pretend not to know what you were saying, but to tell you the truth, I wasn't sure if I trusted you yet."

He looked her up and down, meaningfully. "I reckon you must figure I'm trustworthy now."

She had the good grace to look embarrassed. "Of course, I do. I should have before. After all, you risked your life to save me from those men." She reached out and touched his arm. "I'm sorry."

Fargo wasn't sure he was ready to accept her apology just yet. Instead, he said, "You *are* an Indian, aren't you?"

"Yes. I am of the Bannock tribe."

Fargo nodded. The markings and decorations on her dress had been vaguely familiar, although he hadn't been able to pin down which tribe they represented. Once a proud people who had hunted throughout the Rocky Mountains, the Bannocks had declined in number until now there were fewer than a thousand of them left, or so Fargo had heard. Like many tribes, they had been hit hard by smallpox epidemics in the first twenty or thirty years after the coming of the white man.

"How'd you come to speak English so well, and to get a white woman's name?" Fargo asked.

One of the braids had fallen forward over Elizabeth's shoulder. She pushed it back with a flip of her hand and said, "I was adopted, along with my younger brother, by a trader and his wife who fancied themselves as missionaries and teachers as well. The rest of our band had fallen sick and died from a fever. My brother and I were ill, too, and would have perished if Angus and Mary McAllister had not come along and nursed us back to health. Since that day, we have been with him. Mary passed away a few years ago. They allowed us to keep some of our Indian ways, but they also gave us new names. Mary taught us to read and speak English so that we might study the white man's Good Book with them."

That made sense to Fargo. The first white men in the mountains had been fur trappers, back in what the old-timers called the "Shining Times." Hard on their heels had come missionaries, bound and determined to convert the heathens into good Christians. They had been out here ever since, spreading the Gospel. From the sound of what Elizabeth had just told him,

17

Angus McAllister had combined the fur trade with missionary work.

"I've heard of a trading post run by a man named McAllister, but I've never been there," Fargo said.

Elizabeth nodded. "That is my home. It is west of here, on the Gallatin River."

"That's forty or fifty miles from here," Fargo said with a frown. "What are you doing that far from home?"

Now Elizabeth grew even more serious. "Looking for my brother, Andrew," she said. "He ran away from the trading post."

Fargo saw that the night chill was causing goose bumps to form on her skin. He couldn't help but notice as well how hard her nipples were. That was probably caused by the cold, too . . . at least partially. He pulled the blanket up around her shoulders.

"No need to freeze while we're talking," he said.

"It would be even warmer if you would sit with me," she pointed out.

Fargo slid over beside her and pulled the blanket around himself, too. They sat there, still nude, hips and shoulders brushing companionably, with their backs against the wall of the bluff.

"You were telling me about your brother," Fargo prompted her.

"Andrew is fifteen, five years younger than me. He's a very . . . confused young man. We dress as Bannocks, look like Bannocks, and yet most of the time we live as whites."

"So he doesn't know if he's white or Indian," Fargo guessed.

"Yes. I've accepted that my life is a mixture of the two paths, but Andrew sees the other Indians who come to our father's trading post and wants to be more like them. He is filled with resentment toward our father and blames him for stealing us away from the path we were born to follow."

"A young fella that age is usually a mite rebellious where his pa is concerned," Fargo mused. "I reckon in your brother's case the circumstances just made things worse for him."

Elizabeth nodded. "Yes, that's what I think, too. He decided that he had to try to live completely as an Indian. So he took a horse and rode away. He was going to the plains to kill a buffalo."

"You know that for a fact?" asked Fargo.

"I believe it. He spoke often of doing just that. He said it was the only way to find out who he really is and to prove that he is truly an Indian."

Fargo shook his head. "The Bannocks have never been buffalo hunters. They've always lived in the mountains and hunted there."

"Yes, I know. But Andrew has heard so much about the buffalo . . . he had to see them for himself."

Fargo nodded slowly. As Elizabeth had said, Andrew McAllister sounded like one mixed-up young fella. Born Indian, raised mostly white, he didn't know who or what he was. A boy like that was liable to get almost any crazy notion in his head.

"All right," Fargo said. "Your brother stole a horse—"

"Not stealing, not really," Elizabeth broke in. "The horse was his, given to him by our father."

"Andrew took a horse, then, and rode off to find a buffalo. I'm guessing that when you found out he was gone, you went after him?"

"Of course. Our father was very upset."

"He asked you to go find your brother?"

Elizabeth hesitated before answering. "Not really."

Fargo smiled. "So you ran off, too."

"Only so that I could find Andrew and bring him

home," Elizabeth said as she sat up straighter. "My father can't just leave the trading post. Someone has to take care of it. When I saw how worried he was, I knew it was up to me to go after Andrew."

"You had a horse, too?"

"Of course. I've been riding since I was a little girl."

"What happened to it?"

"He was frightened by a mountain lion," she said with a sigh. "I fell off, and he ran away. I . . . I think the mountain lion got him."

She lowered her head and stared at the ground. Fargo couldn't tell if she was ashamed that she had let herself be thrown, or if she was upset because her horse might have been killed, or some of both. Probably both, he decided.

"That left you on foot," he said. "When do those two men come into the story?"

"Not long after I lost my horse," Elizabeth replied. "I was walking, and I heard hoofbeats. I hoped it was my horse coming back, but then I saw the two white men. They were strangers, and I . . . I didn't trust them."

"You were right about that," Fargo said.

"I tried to run and hide before they saw me, but I didn't make it into the trees in time. I knew they were coming after me, and I was afraid of them . . . of what they might do to me."

Scorn dripped from her voice as she went on. "I've seen the way white men look at me when they come to the trading post. None of them would bother me there because of my father, but since I was alone, I knew nothing would stop them." She turned and looked at Fargo. "I was wrong about that. You stopped them, Skye."

"I gave them more than one chance to ride on," Fargo said grimly. "It was their choice to push things."

They were silent for a few moments. Then Fargo

spoke again. "Do you know if there were any more of them?"

"The white men, you mean?" Elizabeth shook her head. "I saw only the two who chased me in to the woods. They could have been traveling with a larger party, though, for all I know."

"Or they might have been alone." Fargo tugged idly on his earlobe as he frowned in thought. "They didn't really look like trappers. A few ranchers have brought herds up here and moved in over east, on the plains, but those two didn't strike me as being cowboys, either. They looked more like owlhoots."

"They were bad men—I know that much. They would have attacked me."

"And likely killed you when they were finished with you," Fargo said bluntly. He felt a shiver go through Elizabeth.

"I hope they were alone," she said. "I hope the one you shot bleeds to death. I know that as a Christian I should not feel this way, but I do." She looked at him. "I fear that I'm still a savage at heart, Skye."

Fargo chuckled. "I've known a lot of so-called savages who were just as decent as civilized folks. More so, in a lot of cases."

Elizabeth rested a hand on Fargo's bare thigh. "And I know some of my father's teachings never made sense to me. I'm still a wanton heathen . . . when I wish to be."

Fargo turned toward her. Her hand closed around his shaft, which had grown hard again from cuddling with her under the blanket while both of them were naked as jaybirds.

He pushed the blanket back a little so that he could lean over and draw one of her nipples into his mouth. He sucked on it and nipped at it with his teeth, and she began to pump harder on his member.

After a moment, Fargo lifted her and turned her so that she was facing him. She straddled his hips and lowered herself onto his erect organ. He slipped easily into her since she was still wet from their previous bout.

She sank down until she was sitting on his thighs and his shaft was buried completely inside her. They sat there like that for a while, not moving, content to simply share the luxuriousness of being joined together as closely as a man and a woman can possibly be.

Then, slowly, Elizabeth began to move, rocking her hips back and forth so that Fargo's hardness slid in and out of her. The movements gradually became harder and faster. Fargo cupped her breasts and stroked the nipples. Elizabeth jerked against him and cried out as she began to climax. Fargo let go, too, erupting inside her.

As her spasms faded, she slumped against him, out of breath again. He put his arms around her and held her, and they both dozed off that way, with him still inside her.

Although that small portion of his brain that was always on guard remained alert for any warning sounds of trouble during the night, Fargo slept soundly. He woke up early the next morning with the smells of coffee and bacon wafting around him, a mouthwatering mixture that brought him fully awake and made him sit up and throw the blanket back.

Elizabeth had built the fire up again. She knelt beside it, cooking bacon in Fargo's frying pan. The small coffeepot from his saddlebags sat at the edge of the flames, steam rising from it. Clearly, she had helped herself to his supplies. Fargo was normally a private man who didn't like folks poking around in his gear, but in this case he could forgive the intrusion.

She was wearing the buckskin dress again, but her hair was loose and unbraided now, hanging far down her back in thick black waves. Her face glowed from a recent scrubbing in cold water. Fargo thought she was beautiful.

She smiled at him across the fire. "Good morning. I thought you were going to sleep the day away."

Fargo squinted at the rosy eastern sky. "The sun's not even up yet."

"It will be soon. And for some reason, you strike me as an early riser, Skye."

That was true enough, thought Fargo. Except on rare occasions, he was usually up before the sun. No reason for today to be any different.

His breath fogged in the chilly morning air as he got up and pulled his clothes on. After checking on the Ovaro, he came back to the fire and hunkered down beside it, enjoying the warmth that came from the flames.

"What am I going to do now, Skye?" Elizabeth asked. "I have to find my brother."

"I know," Fargo said with a nod. "That's why I'm going to help you look for him."

Her face lit up with a smile. "You will? I was hoping you would, but I didn't want to ask you. . . ."

"Would've been fine if you had," Fargo told her, "but I don't mind volunteering, either." He grew more solemn as he went on. "I've got to tell you, though, I'm not sure it's a good idea to drag him back to your father's trading post."

"But he has to come back! Father's worried about him—"

"If Andrew's got it in his head that he has to go

off and hunt a buffalo to prove something to himself, nothing else is going to satisfy him. Sure, maybe we can force him to go back to the trading post with you, but he's liable to run off again just as soon as he gets another chance."

"I suppose you're right . . . but why can't he just be reasonable?"

Fargo laughed. "White or Indian, it doesn't matter. It's probably even the same on the other side of the world in China. Fifteen-year-old boys and being reasonable are just two things that don't really go together."

"Well, they should," Elizabeth said with an exasperated sigh.

Fargo didn't have an answer for that, so he said instead, "That bacon smells mighty good."

He had some biscuits in his saddlebags that he had cooked a couple of days earlier, so they ate those along with the bacon. They washed down the food with strong, hot coffee. Fargo had only one cup, so they shared it. After everything they had shared the night before, it seemed only appropriate.

When they were finished with breakfast and had cleaned up, Fargo saddled the Ovaro. "You reckon you could find the place where you lost your horse?" he asked Elizabeth. "My stallion can carry double for a while, but it would be better if we each had a mount."

"I'll try," she said doubtfully. "I'm not that familiar with this part of the country. Anyway, I'm afraid that mountain lion got my horse."

"We don't know that," Fargo pointed out. "Maybe he got away and we can round him up."

"I suppose it's possible. . . . That'll mean going back to the area where those two men started chasing me, though."

"I'm hoping the one who was wounded is long gone

by now. And if we're going to find your brother, we'll have to go back in that direction anyway."

Elizabeth nodded. "That's true. I was able to follow his trail for a while, but I had lost it not long before I lost my horse. Maybe you can find—" She stopped short and stared at him. "Skye Fargo! I knew your name was familiar. You're the one they call the Trailsman!"

"Guilty as charged," Fargo admitted with a grin.

"Then you *can* find Andrew's trail. I'm sure of it now."

Fargo wasn't that confident. He was good at what he did, no doubt about that, but he was no miracle worker. He would do his best—that was all.

He mounted up and helped Elizabeth climb onto the Ovaro behind him. They left the camp and rode east again, doubling back on the route they had followed the day before.

Fargo kept his eyes open, remaining alert for any sign of trouble. He couldn't help but be aware, though, of how nice it felt to have Elizabeth's breasts pressed against his back. Wherever they wound up that night, he hoped he would have the opportunity to get to know that lush, warm body of hers even better than he already did.

Elizabeth remembered a few landmarks she had seen the previous day. She directed Fargo to an area about a mile away from the spot where he had been camped when he first encountered her. Looking around as they entered a long, parklike meadow, she said, "I think this is where I ran into the mountain lion." She pointed to a clump of boulders at the edge of the meadow. "He came out of there. My horse threw me and then galloped off that way"—she pointed again, toward the far end of the meadow—"with the lion chasing it."

"You're lucky that big cat didn't come after you," Fargo said. "He must've had a hankering for horse-flesh."

Elizabeth shuddered a little. "I know. I'm not sure what I would have done if that beast had attacked me."

"Did you set out to find your brother without a gun or any other kind of weapon?"

"I had a rifle and a knife," she said, "but they were both on the horse."

"So you were left without any way to defend your-self when the horse ran off."

"That's right. That's why I tried to get away from those men." She gave a little toss of her head, which made the long black hair swirl around her shoulders. "If I'd had my rifle, I would have shot both of them before they could ever get near me."

"I'll bet you would have," Fargo said with a grin.

"But since I wasn't armed, I ran into the trees over there"—she pointed at a thick stand of pine and fir trees—"then over that hill and along a ridge and fi-nally through the trees where you were camped."

"Must have been pretty close to a mile," Fargo commented. "That's a pretty long run, especially with a couple of men chasing you on horseback."

"I could make better time through the trees on foot than they could on their horses. Anyway, I've always been a good runner."

Many Indians were, Fargo thought. The Apaches, down in Arizona Territory, could sometimes run a horse right into the ground.

"I managed to stay ahead of them," Elizabeth went on. "But they would have caught me sooner or later, if I hadn't stumbled onto your camp, Skye. I owe you my life."

"I'm just glad I was in the right place at the right

time to help out," Fargo said. "And the way I see it, you don't owe me anything."

"I see it differently," Elizabeth murmured.

Fargo didn't comment on that. He just sent the Ovaro trotting easily across the meadow where Elizabeth had run in to the mountain lion. He was already more optimistic that they might find her horse. There were no buzzards circling in the sky overhead, as there might have been if there was a fresh horse carcass somewhere nearby.

A few minutes later, the Ovaro stopped and let out a neigh. There was an answering nicker from the trees. A brown gelding trotted into view.

"There he is!" Elizabeth exclaimed. "Skye, you were right! He got away from the mountain lion!"

"A horse can sometimes fight off a big cat," Fargo said. "Let's go see if he's hurt."

The gelding had some deep scratches on his right flank where the mountain lion had clawed him. Those seemed to be the horse's only injuries. Once Fargo had smeared some medicinal ointment on them, he thought the gashes would probably heal up all right. The horse wasn't hurt so badly that he couldn't carry Elizabeth.

She hugged the animal's neck, clearly glad to see him. "My luck is holding," she told Fargo with a smile.

"Let's hope that continues. Now, can you show me where you were when you lost your brother's trail?"

She swung up onto the gelding, which still wore its saddle. "That way," she said, and sent the horse trotting off to the southwest.

Finding Andrew McAllister's trail proved to be more difficult than locating the gelding had been. It took most of the morning before Elizabeth found some tracks and pointed them out to Fargo.

"There," she said. "I'm certain those were the hoofprints I was following."

Fargo studied the sign for a moment and frowned. "Those tracks were left by an unshod pony. Your horse is wearing shoes, as well as that saddle."

"I told you, Andrew wants to live completely as an Indian. He refused to ride a shod horse, so Father got that pony for him from a band of friendly Shoshone. He doesn't use a saddle, either, only a blanket pad."

Fargo nodded, accepting her explanation. He got down from the Ovaro and knelt beside the hoofprints, studying them intently for long moments until he knew everything about them. Now if he ever saw the same tracks somewhere else, he would recognize them instantly.

He mounted up again and rode along slowly, following the trail. Elizabeth rode after him. When they reached a stretch of rocky ground a short time later, she said, "This is where I lost the trail, Skye. I couldn't find any more hoofprints."

"You were looking at the ground," Fargo said. "Look at the bushes and the trees. See the way that branch has been bent back and cracked a little? And there's a hair from a horse's tail caught on that branch over there." They rode a little farther. "Something rubbed against that tree trunk there, see?"

"It seems so simple when you do it." Elizabeth shook her head. "I'm not much of a tracker."

In a way, Angus McAllister hadn't done his adopted children any favors in the way he had raised them, thought Fargo. An Indian should have been able to read signs better than that. If Elizabeth was any indication, then she and her brother really were of two worlds. Yet, at the same time, they truly belonged to neither.

Fargo could see why that would have bothered Andrew McAllister. But he wasn't looking for Andrew so that he could help the young man figure out how to live his life. Andrew would have to muddle through that age-old dilemma on his own. Fargo just wanted to find him and try to talk him into returning to the trading post, so that Elizabeth would go back to where she was relatively safe.

Fargo had no trouble following the trail. To his keen, experienced eyes, it might as well have been deliberately blazed. Andrew's tracks led east, away from the mountains and toward the vast, gently rolling prairie where seemingly endless herds of buffalo darkened the landscape.

Fargo and Elizabeth paused in the middle of the day and made a quick lunch of bacon and biscuits left over from their breakfast. Then they pushed on.

Fargo had kept his eyes open but hadn't seen any other humans. He was curious about what had happened to the other man he'd shot, but he wasn't the sort to go looking for trouble. It found him often enough on its own.

Around midafternoon, Fargo suddenly reined in and motioned for Elizabeth to do likewise. He swung down from the saddle and held on to the Ovaro's reins as he studied the ground.

"What is it, Skye?" Elizabeth asked anxiously. "Have you lost the trail?"

"No, it's still here," Fargo said. He lifted a hand and pointed off to the east. "Andrew's still heading toward the plains. But here's something different." He indicated some other tracks that were faint but visible coming from the north. "More riders on shod horses. White men."

"Do you think they could have been with the man you wounded yesterday?"

Fargo shook his head. "No way of knowing. I didn't study those hoofprints closely enough to know if any of these came from that man's horse. But here's what concerns me." He waved a hand toward the route that Andrew had taken. "These men . . . four of them, I'd say . . . came along shortly after Andrew had ridden through here. They were heading south, but they stopped and turned east instead. See how some of their tracks are on top of the ones Andrew's pony left?"

"They're following him!" Elizabeth exclaimed as she realized what Fargo was getting at.

He nodded. "That's sure what it looks like."

"Could they have seen him and decided to follow him?"

"That's certainly possible."

"Why would they do that?"

"Don't know," said Fargo. "And I reckon there's only one way to find out."

He mounted up again and sent the stallion trotting along the trail left by Andrew McAllister and the mysterious white men. His worry increased as he saw that the stride of Andrew's pony had lengthened and so had the strides of the other horses.

Andrew had spotted the men following him and had tried to get away. The other four riders had given chase. Those were the only conclusions Fargo could draw from the evidence he saw on the ground.

He didn't say anything about that to Elizabeth, however. She was already worried enough about her brother. There was no point in making her worry even more until they found out exactly what had been the outcome of the race between Andrew and his four pursuers.

A short time later, in an open area between some trees, Fargo saw a welter of hoofprints all jumbled up together. He knew this was the spot where the men had caught up to Andrew. Evidently, there had been quite a commotion here. To Fargo's eyes, it looked as if the men had surrounded Andrew and forced him to stop.

Then he saw something else that made him haul back on the reins and drop to the ground almost before the Ovaro had stopped moving. "Skye, what is it?" Elizabeth asked as Fargo went down on one knee and studied a patch of grass. It had been pushed down as if something heavy had fallen on it. Fargo touched several blades of grass and then looked at the dark red stain on his fingertips.

He couldn't keep this from her. She was the boy's sister and deserved the truth . . . even though he didn't know exactly what had happened.

"There was some trouble here," he said. "Looks like a struggle of some sort. I'd say those men caught up to Andrew, and he put up a fight when they surrounded him."

"What's that on your fingers, Skye?" Her voice trembled a little as she asked the question.

Fargo met her gaze squarely as he said, "It's blood. There's blood on the grass."

3

It was hard to tell because of her coppery skin, but Fargo thought Elizabeth went pale at his statement. After a moment, she said, "You . . . you don't know that it's Andrew's blood."

"That's true," Fargo agreed. "There's no way of knowing who it belongs to. But somebody was hurt here, and your brother was outnumbered four to one."

"That doesn't mean anything. Andrew . . . Andrew has always been a scrapper, as Father puts it. He could have bloodied the nose of one of those men."

Or they could have shot him off his pony, thought Fargo, but he didn't say that. Elizabeth was worried enough already. Instead, he looked around, studying the marks on the ground, and then pointed.

"All five horses headed off to the east together," he said. "And they're all carrying riders, which means that Andrew went with the men."

Fargo hoped that Andrew hadn't ridden off strapped belly down over his horse. He mounted the Ovaro.

"All right, then, we can follow them and find out what happened," Elizabeth said.

"If that fella I ventilated is with them, they're liable not to be too happy to see us," Fargo pointed out.

Elizabeth's face was set in stubborn lines. "I don't care. I have to find out what happened to Andrew."

Fargo hadn't expected anything less from her. He nodded and said, "Let's go. But when we catch up to them, we'll approach carefully and try to find out what the situation is before they know we're anywhere near."

She sighed. "You're right, of course. If they're holding Andrew prisoner, it might just make things worse if we come riding in and demand that they let him go."

"Now you're thinking," Fargo said as he heeled the Ovaro into a trot. Elizabeth fell in beside him.

They rode with an added urgency now. Four white men and one lone Indian boy wasn't a good combination. A lot of whites bore a grudge against all Indians, sometimes with good reason. During the decades of westward expansion, there had been plenty of bloodshed on both sides.

They were several miles south of the Yellowstone River, traveling in a generally easterly direction through foothills that rose to another range of mountains farther south. Fargo had been through this country several times, so it wasn't new to him. He knew there were no settlements or trading posts in the area. Angus McAllister's trading post over on the Gallatin River was probably the closest bit of civilization that could be found.

They had been following the tracks for about an hour when several gunshots rang out ahead of them. Fargo hauled back on the reins, bringing the stallion to a halt. Beside him, Elizabeth reined in as well.

"Those were shots, Skye," she said.

Fargo nodded. "I know. Maybe half a mile away. Sound travels pretty well in this thin air." About four hundred yards away, there was a wooded ridge in front of them. Fargo pointed toward it and said, "They came from the other side of that ridge."

There had been no more shots since that brief flurry. Elizabeth leaned forward in the saddle and said, "We have to find out what's going on over there. Andrew could be in trouble."

Fargo thought that was pretty likely. He glanced over at Elizabeth and asked, "I don't reckon there's any chance of you waiting here while I take a look, is there?"

Her jaw was taut as she shook her head. "I'm going with you."

Fargo nodded curtly. He could have insisted that she stay behind, but short of pulling her off her horse and hog-tying her, he didn't see any way he could enforce that edict. Besides, it might be better to have her with him so that he could keep an eye on her.

"Let's go," he said.

He put the Ovaro into a run. The big stallion could have easily outdistanced Elizabeth's mount, but Fargo held the Ovaro in a little so that he didn't run off and leave her. They covered the distance to the ridge quickly. Fargo slowed down and rode up the wooded slope, weaving among the pines and fir and spruce.

He stopped before he reached the top of the ridge. Elizabeth followed suit. As Fargo swung down from the saddle, he said quietly, "We'll leave the horses here and go ahead on foot. Stay close to me, and try not to make any noise."

"I can be quiet," she said, sounding a little offended. "I *am* an Indian, after all."

Well, she was sort of an Indian, thought Fargo, but he didn't bother saying as much. Instead, he tied the

Ovaro's reins to a sapling and started toward the crest of the ridge. Elizabeth followed him.

When they reached the top, Fargo went to a knee and motioned for Elizabeth to do likewise. He leaned forward behind some screening brush and parted a couple of branches. From here, he could see down the far side of the ridge to the little valley beyond.

He had already smelled smoke and knew that the four men had built a campfire. There were still several hours of light left in the day, and Fargo was somewhat surprised that anybody would make camp this early. They must have had a reason for that.

The men had stopped beside a narrow, tree-lined creek. One man was tending the fire, while another saw to the horses. The other two stood in front of one of the trees on the creekbank.

Elizabeth's hand clutched Fargo's arm. Her fingers dug hard into his flesh through the sleeve of his buckskin shirt when she saw the figure tied to the tree.

Fargo knew he was looking at Andrew McAllister. The young man had the same thick, dark hair and bronzed skin as his sister. He wore moccasins, buckskin leggings, and a tunic decorated with elaborate beadwork. His head drooped forward as if he were unconscious. Fargo saw a crimson smear of blood on his face.

Other than the gash on his forehead that had produced that blood, Andrew didn't seem to be hurt. That wasn't going to last, though. One of the men grasped the young man's hair, jerked his head up, and slammed a fist into his face.

Elizabeth gasped and squeezed Fargo's arm even harder. "My God!" she exclaimed. "They're beating him!"

Fargo shushed her as the other man stepped up and drove his fist into Andrew's stomach. The young man would have doubled over in pain if he had been able to, but the rope tied around him held him upright against the tree trunk.

"Skye, we've got to stop them!" Elizabeth hissed. "They're going to kill him! Do something!"

Fargo knew he could fetch his Henry rifle from its saddle sheath and down two or three of Andrew's captors before the men knew what was going on. He might even be able to kill all four of them. But that would amount to little more than cold-blooded murder, and Fargo had never been the sort of man to resort to that. He didn't kill unless he had to, and then he did it facing his enemies.

"Stay up here on the ridge, out of sight," he said as he straightened and started back toward the horses. "I'll ride down and see if I can pull your brother out of this mess."

"I should go with you—"

"No, you shouldn't," Fargo said curtly. "If those hombres see you, it'll just complicate things. Stay out of sight unless something happens to me."

"What do I do then?" Elizabeth asked as they reached the horses.

Fargo pulled the Henry from its scabbard. "Do you know how to handle a rifle?"

"Yes, I've been hunting many times with my father and Andrew." She stared at the repeater. "I've never seen a rifle quite like that one, though."

"It's a fairly new model." Fargo showed her how to work the lever and throw a cartridge into the firing chamber. "It holds fifteen shots. Load it on Sunday and shoot it all week, some folks say," he added with a grim smile. Then he handed the rifle to her. "If I go down, you'll have to do whatever you think is best."

She nodded nervously. "Be careful, Skye," she urged him.

"I intend to be," he said. Then he swung up into the saddle and rode over the crest of the ridge.

He didn't hurry as he started down the slope toward the camp. The men were busy with the fire, the horses, and beating Andrew. None of them had noticed him yet, and Fargo didn't see any point in calling attention to himself. Since he was now armed with just his Colt and the Arkansas toothpick, he wanted to get as close as he could before they noticed him.

His jaw clenched in anger as the two men continued hitting Andrew. From the way the young man's head drooped loosely on his neck, Fargo could tell that he was only half-conscious, at best. He might be out cold by now.

That proved to be the case, because one of the men said loudly enough for Fargo to hear, "The redskin's passed out. I'll get some water to throw in his face and bring him around."

As the man turned away from the tree where Andrew was tied, he saw Fargo riding toward the camp. The man stopped short, stiffening in surprise.

"Hey! Somebody's comin'!"

Fargo was only about fifty yards away now. He kept the Ovaro moving forward at an easy walk.

The four men stayed spread out as they stepped forward to intercept Fargo. The two who had been beating Andrew were to his left; the one by the fire was almost directly in front of him; and the man who had been tending to the horses was a short distance off to the right. Fargo would have preferred that they were bunched up, but he would just have to deal with the situation the way it was.

He reined the Ovaro to a halt when he was about forty feet from the men. Giving them what he hoped would pass for a friendly nod, he said, "Howdy. I see you've got you an Indian."

"That's right," one of the men on Fargo's left replied. "What damn business is it of yours?"

"Didn't say it was any of my business. Just making a comment."

Fargo sat casually in the saddle, seemingly at ease, and only mildly interested in what he saw in front of him. His eyes were actually appraising the four men he faced. They were all cut from the same cloth as the two men who had chased Elizabeth the day before: hard-featured, heavily armed gents who looked like they wouldn't back down from any trouble. Fargo didn't see the man he had wounded among them.

"We're not interested in your comments," said the man who seemed to be the spokesman. "If you've got any sense, you'll ride on. You ain't wanted here."

Fargo frowned a little. "Not very hospitable, are you, mister? Out here on the frontier, if a stranger rides up, the least you can do is offer to share your fire and your coffee."

"We ain't interested in bein' hospitable," the man said. He rested his hand on the butt of the gun at his hip. "Now ride on."

Fargo ignored the command and inclined his head toward Andrew. "How come you're beating up that Indian boy? He try to lift your scalp?"

"That's none of your business, either."

The other man who had been handing out the beating laughed. "As if one Injun could scalp any of us," he said with a sneer. "And this un's just a young buck, at that."

"Shut up, Baird," snapped the first man.

"You shut up, Prescott," the second man came right back. "Nobody made you the boss o' this outfit."

The men glared at each other, which meant they weren't looking at Fargo. The other two still were, though. In fact, they were watching him like hawks.

"You better be careful," Fargo said. "If you treat that boy bad, the rest of his tribe is liable to come after you. There's not much Indian trouble in these parts right now, but you never can tell when things will blow up again."

The man called Baird was still sneering. "We ain't afraid of a few Injuns. When the rest of our bunch gets here, those red savages wouldn't dare bother us."

So there were more men coming, thought Fargo. That bit of news supported his hunch that the two men from the day before had been part of a larger group. He wondered what a gang of hardcases was doing in the area. They were bound to be up to no good.

But right now, his main concern was Andrew. He said, "I'd let the boy go, just to be sure."

Prescott snarled, "You don't take advice too well, do you, mister?"

"Nope," Fargo drawled. "Never have. Don't reckon I ever will."

"You got a name?"

"It's Fargo. Skye Fargo."

It didn't mean anything to Prescott or Baird, or to the man at the fire. But the one who stood not far from the horses stiffened and exclaimed, "The Trailsman!"

Prescott glanced at him. "Who?"

"He's the Trailsman," the other man said. "Fella who's done a lot of scouting for the army and other folks. Supposed to be the best there is at following sign." The man's voice got a nervous edge to it as he added, "Supposed to be mighty damn fast with a gun, too."

Prescott looked at Fargo with new interest. "Is that true, mister?"

Fargo shrugged. "I've been called the Trailsman, all

right, and I've scouted for the army. As for the rest of it . . . well, I guess you'd have to find that out for yourself."

Prescott's face was taut with anger. He didn't like being challenged. But he had a new respect for Fargo and he said, "There's four of us."

"That's right," Fargo said calmly. "I can count."

Prescott's eyes narrowed in suspicion. "Who's that Indian kid to you? How come you really want us to let him go?"

"I never saw him before until I rode down that hill," Fargo answered. "I don't like seeing anyone being beaten who's tied up and defenseless. That just rubs me the wrong way."

"He tried to steal our horses," Prescott said. "We got a right to deal with a horse thief however we see fit, don't we?"

Fargo knew that was a lie. Andrew had been riding along peacefully, heading for the plains to hunt a buffalo, when these four men had gotten on his trail. They had followed him, surrounded him, and probably knocked him off his horse by pistol-whipping him. That would account for the gash on Andrew's forehead and the blood Fargo had found on the grass back along the trail.

"He tried to run off after we made camp," Baird put in. "But he stopped fast enough when the bullets started buzzin' around his ears."

That explained the shots Fargo and Elizabeth had heard. Thinking of Elizabeth made Fargo want to look up toward the ridge and be certain she was staying out of sight, but he knew he couldn't do that. He didn't want to give away her presence to these men.

"So I'll tell you again," Prescott said. "This is none of your business, Fargo. You need to ride on. We ain't lookin' for trouble, but we ain't lettin' the boy go. And like I said, there's four of us and only one of you."

The man by the horses said, "Prescott, I ain't hankerin' to swap lead with the Trailsman. This is your fight, not mine."

"Barnett, you damned coward," Prescott grated. "I ain't gonna forget this—"

Before he could go on, a shot rang out from the ridge behind Fargo. The bullet kicked up dirt just in front of Prescott and Baird, making them jump backward. Fargo didn't know what the hell Elizabeth thought she was doing by opening fire, but it was too late now. With lightning speed, he drew his Colt and covered the man by the fire and the one called Barnett.

"Don't move!" he snapped. "Baird, Prescott, keep your hands away from your guns or my partners up there on the ridge will put the next ones right in your gizzards!"

All four of the hardcases stood tensely, their hands half lifted. Fargo hoped like hell Elizabeth was a good enough shot to get Prescott or Baird, or both, if a gun battle broke out. If she wasn't, he was in a bad position. He figured he could bring down all four of the men if he had to, but they would get lead into him, too.

"You're makin' a bad mistake, Fargo," Prescott hissed at him.

"You made the mistake when you jumped that boy," Fargo replied. He gestured with the barrel of the Colt. "All of you get over by the fire."

Bunching them up would put him at less of a disadvantage. They had to realize that, but they didn't know how many men were hidden up on the ridge, nor how accurate their rifle fire would be. They sure as hell didn't know there was only one young, relatively inexperienced woman up there!

So Prescott, Baird, and Barnett reluctantly moved toward the fire, joining the fourth man there. Keeping them covered with the Colt, Fargo rode around them to the tree where Andrew was starting to come around. The young man let out a groan and tried to lift his head.

"Take it easy," Fargo told him. He dismounted, keeping the stallion between him and the four hard-cases, and keeping the revolver pointed at them as well. He stepped over to the tree, shifted the Colt to his left hand, and bent slightly to draw the Arkansas toothpick from the sheath on his calf. It took only a couple of slashes with the razor-sharp blade to cut the ropes holding Andrew to the tree trunk.

As soon as he was freed, the young man fell to his knees. Fargo managed to grab his shirt with the hand that was holding the big knife. The muscles in Fargo's arm and shoulder bunched and corded as he hauled the semiconscious Bannock youngster onto his feet.

"Come on," he said. He walked Andrew over to the Ovaro. At Fargo's urging, Andrew hung on to the saddle horn and supported himself that way for a moment while Fargo sheathed the toothpick. Then Fargo said, "Get on the horse."

He had to repeat the command before it soaked in Andrew's brain enough for the young man to act on it. He was still mostly dazed. Awkwardly, Andrew pulled himself into the saddle and slumped there.

"Ride to the top of that ridge," Fargo told him without taking his eyes off the four men under his gun. "Somebody will be waiting for you."

Andrew looked blearily at him. "I . . . don't know you," the young man said.

"I'm a friend," Fargo said. "Just go."

Clumsily, Andrew took up the reins. He banged his heels against the stallion's sides. The Ovaro didn't budge until Fargo slapped him lightly on the rump. Then the horse started for the top of the ridge. Andrew swayed and bounced in the saddle. Fargo hoped he wouldn't fall off before he reached Elizabeth.

Fargo moved around so that he could cover the four men and watch Andrew ride up the slope at the same time. He saw Andrew reach the top and dismount. It was more like falling off, actually. As soon as Andrew was off the horse, Fargo gave a shrill whistle. The Ovaro wheeled around and came trotting back down the hill, answering his master's summons.

"Mister, you're gonna be damned sorry you ever crossed our trail," Prescott said.

"I'm already sorry. Running into the likes of you is enough to put a bad taste in my mouth all day."

Prescott glared murderously at him, but didn't say anything else. When the Ovaro reached him, Fargo mounted up without holstering the gun.

"The men on top of that ridge are crack shots," Fargo said. "Unbuckle your gun belts, slow and easy, and lay them on the ground."

"Damn it!" Baird burst out. "You can't leave us unarmed out here in the middle of the wilderness!"

"I'm not going to take your guns," Fargo told him. "But I'm not going to ride up that hill and let you shoot me in the back, either. Now shuck those hoglegs."

Grudgingly, with a lot of curses muttered under their breaths, the four men unfastened their gun belts and laid them on the ground.

"Now get across the creek," Fargo ordered.

"We'll get our feet wet," Barnett protested.

"They'll dry," Fargo assured the man. "Get moving."

Still cursing, the four men waded across the creek.

The current was fast and the water had to be cold due to the snowmelt higher in the mountains, but the stream was still fairly shallow. The men had no trouble crossing.

"Keep moving," Fargo called to them.

They trudged along until they were at least a hundred yards away from the creek. Fargo holstered his Colt at last, rode over to the horses that belonged to the four hardcases, and jerked loose the pickets to which the animals were tied. He got a firm grip on the rope hackamore worn by Andrew's pony.

Then he took his hat off, waved it over his head, and shouted. The other horses stampeded, galloping off along the creek. Fargo didn't figure they would stop for at least a quarter of a mile, maybe more. The men on the other side of the creek yelled furiously as they saw their mounts running away.

Leading Andrew's pony, Fargo wheeled the Ovaro and touched its flanks lightly with his boot heels. The stallion leaped into a gallop. Fargo would be over the ridge and long gone with Elizabeth and Andrew before the men could get their guns and round up their horses. He wasn't worried about immediate pursuit.

When he topped the ridge, he was glad to see that Elizabeth had gotten Andrew mounted on her horse. The young man seemed a bit more coherent now. Elizabeth tossed the Henry to Fargo and then swung up behind her brother. She reached around him to hold him on and handle the reins.

Fargo caught the rifle and slid it back in its sheath. He kept moving, waving for Elizabeth to follow him.

They rode hard for the next half hour, putting a lot of distance between themselves and the four hardcases. When Fargo judged they were safe, he reined in and signaled a halt. Elizabeth pulled up beside him.

Andrew was fully conscious now. The cool air blowing in his face as they raced along had taken care of that. He looked over at Fargo and asked, "Who are you, mister? What are you doing with my sister?"

"I reckon you were still out of your head when I introduced myself to those boys back there," Fargo said. "My name is Skye Fargo. I'm a friend of Elizabeth's."

Andrew turned his head to look back at his sister. "I know why you're here," he said accusingly. "You want me to go home."

"Father is very worried about you, Andrew," she said. "I was, too. I still am. You're hurt." She reached up to touch the dried blood on his face.

He swatted her hand away. "I'm all right. Leave me alone."

"You weren't all right when those men were whaling away on you," Fargo pointed out. "Maybe they would have stopped before they beat you to death, but they intended on handing you a big dose of pain—that's for sure."

"Those bastards," Andrew grated out. "I didn't do anything to them. They just rode up behind me and started chasing me."

"We know," Fargo said with a nod. "I could read the sign. They claimed you tried to steal their horses, but I knew that was a lie."

"I'm not a thief!"

"Of course, you're not," Elizabeth said. "But you were very thoughtless when you ran away from the trading post."

"Listen to you!" Andrew cried. "You don't even sound like an Indian!"

"We are what we are," his sister said.

Most people couldn't argue with such a simple, obvious piece of logic. But a fifteen-year-old boy could argue with just about anything, logical or not, Fargo mused.

He changed the subject by asking Elizabeth, "How come you fired that shot while I was talking to those men?"

There was a touch of defensiveness in her voice as she answered, as if she had been waiting for him to scold her. "I thought one of them was trying to sneak his gun out. Besides, I could hear enough of what they were saying to know that they weren't going to cooperate with you unless they were threatened."

"Well, it seems like you're a pretty good shot," Fargo told her, "and I reckon it worked out all right. The way it was going, it probably would have come down to shooting sooner or later. If we run into more trouble, though, you need to do what I tell you to do."

She didn't say anything, just tossed her long dark hair a little. Fargo looked away so that she wouldn't see the grin that came over his face at her show of defiance.

"You're just like the whites," Andrew said to his sister. "You talk and talk. I won't go back. I'm going to hunt a buffalo." He slid down from the horse and reached for the reins of his pony.

Fargo held on to them. "Seems to me that after we went to all the trouble of getting you away from those hombres, the least you could do is go along with what your sister wants."

"You don't know anything about it!" Andrew glared up at Fargo.

"He knows all about it," Elizabeth said. "I told him."

He turned his glower toward her. "What else did you do with him?"

Elizabeth surprised Fargo then. She left the saddle

in a diving tackle that took Andrew around the waist and carried him to the ground. They started to wrestle. Elizabeth slapped at Andrew, saying, "How dare you! How dare you!"

They were fighting just like a pair of white siblings, Fargo thought. He had seen young Indian kids do the same, but never a brother and sister who were pretty much grown like these two. Shaking his head, he dismounted and reached down to grab their shirts. He jerked them up and pulled them apart, holding them out at arm's length from each other.

"Take it easy!" he told them. "You two go to scrapping like a couple of catamounts and there's no telling what'll happen. We're wasting time, and those men could be trailing us right now."

That made Elizabeth stop struggling, and a second later Andrew followed suit. Elizabeth looked at Fargo and said, "You really think so?"

"We don't know that they're not coming after us." Fargo looked at Andrew and asked, "Did you hear them say anything about who they are or what they're doing out here?"

The sharply worded question cut through Andrew's anger and resentment and made him frown in thought. After a moment, he shook his head and said, "Not really. They called each other by name, and they mentioned another man named Ollie or Olney or something like that. I know they were part of a larger group, but I don't remember anything else. I . . . I don't really remember much of anything after they chased me down and the one called Prescott hit me with his gun."

At that, Elizabeth forgot her anger, too, and was immediately solicitous again, saying, "We need to clean that cut on your forehead, Andrew."

"It'll have to wait," Fargo said. "We need to get

moving again. How about it, Andrew? Are you willing to go back to your father's trading post without a fight?"

For a long moment, the young man didn't say anything. Finally, he sighed and nodded. "I suppose so. Elizabeth will never let me hear the end of it if I don't."

"That's right," she agreed. "I won't."

"Come on, then," Fargo said. "Mount up, both of you. And no more fighting."

They didn't make any promises to that effect, but they did get back on their horses and fall in beside Fargo. They rode west, toward the Gallatin River and the trading post owned by Angus McAllister.

4

Fargo kept a watchful eye behind them as they traveled west during the rest of that day, but he didn't see any signs of pursuit. It was possible that Prescott, Baird, and the other two men would decide that coming after them would be too much trouble, not to mention too dangerous.

However, Fargo didn't really expect things to turn out that way. Prescott's pride had been wounded, and he hadn't seemed like the sort of man to forgive and forget. Fargo had humiliated him by disarming him and making him wade across the creek. Prescott would want to settle that score, and likely he would drag the other three along with him.

If Fargo, Elizabeth, and Andrew could reach the trading post, Fargo doubted if the men would attack them there. But if Prescott and the others did attack, the trading post would be easier to defend than if Fargo and his young companions were caught out in the open. So he kept them moving at a fast clip and watched their back trail.

Nightfall found them in the foothills below the Bozeman Pass. The mountains of the Bridger Range rose to the north of the pass; to the south were the peaks of the Gallatin Range. On the far side of the pass was a broad valley. The Gallatin River flowed through that valley, which was one of the prettiest in this part of the country.

A game trail led up to the pass. Fargo knew they couldn't get through the pass before dark, so he decided to camp on the eastern slope. He found a place off the trail, under some trees, where they would be fairly well hidden.

"We'll have to have a cold camp tonight," he informed Elizabeth and Andrew as they dismounted. "We can't risk building a fire."

"You think those men might see it if we did?" Elizabeth asked.

"There's a chance. And taking foolish chances can get you killed out here."

There was enough grass for the horses to graze. Fargo still had some jerky, so the humans would have to make do with that for supper.

The first order of business for Elizabeth, though, was cleaning the gash in Andrew's forehead. It was about three inches long and had bled heavily. When she had washed away the blood, Fargo supplied some of the same ointment he had used on the scratches on Elizabeth's horse. Then he tore a strip of cloth from the tail of a spare homespun shirt and gave it to her to use as a bandage. She tied it around Andrew's head, covering the injury.

As dusk settled down, the three of them sat on a fallen log. They gnawed on the dried, jerked venison. Fargo asked Andrew, "Did you have a gun or any other weapons when you left the trading post?"

"I had a bow and a quiver of arrows," the young man said. "I wanted to hunt the buffalo like my ancestors did." He shook his head. "Those men took them away from me. I don't know what they did with them."

"Maybe you didn't know this, but the Bannock never hunted buffalo much," Fargo said. "Since they dwell in the mountains, they usually go after bear, elk, and moose."

Andrew frowned. "Indians hunt buffalo. It is the way of our people."

The youngster didn't know as much about the way of his people as he thought he did, Fargo reflected. Andrew had gotten some foolish notions in his head, and when he had acted on them, he had come close to getting himself killed. If Andrew had ever actually reached the Great Plains and really tried to get himself a buffalo, chances were he would've wound up getting trampled.

The snowmelt had every little stream and rivulet flowing, so water was no problem. Fargo filled his canteen at a tiny creek, upstream from where the horses drank. When he came back to the camp, he found that Andrew had already wrapped himself in a blanket and stretched out on a makeshift bed of pine boughs. He lay motionless, but his breathing revealed that he had not yet fallen asleep.

Fargo sat down on the log again. Elizabeth slid over close to him and whispered, "There are not enough blankets for all of us. I'll have to share with you, Skye."

There was nothing Fargo would have liked better under different circumstances. He said, "You can have the blanket. I reckon I'll be sitting up all night keeping watch."

"You can't do that," Elizabeth protested. "You need rest, too."

"I'll be all right," Fargo assured her. "I'll probably

catch a catnap or two during the night. This won't be the first time I've stood guard like that."

Besides, he thought, he wouldn't really feel comfortable making love to Elizabeth with her surly brother lying only a few feet away. Fargo preferred his passion a mite more private-like.

He really did want to stay awake most of the night, in case Prescott and the other men tried to sneak up on them. He could count on the Ovaro to let him know if anybody came skulking around, but he wanted to be ready to meet any such threat immediately.

Elizabeth sighed and said, "All right, I suppose I understand. Good night, Skye."

"Good ni—" he started to say, but she leaned over and kissed him before he could finish. Her lips were warm and urgent against his. Instinctively, Fargo slid an arm around her waist and drew her even closer. Her tongue slipped hotly into his mouth.

It would have been easy to get carried away, but Fargo had more self-control than that. After a long moment, he broke the kiss and gently pushed Elizabeth away, putting a little distance between them. "You'd better get some rest," he told her quietly. "I'd like to reach the trading post tomorrow, so that'll make for a long day's ride."

"You're right," she said in a disappointed tone. She stood up, took the extra blanket, and bedded down not far from her brother. Fargo remained seated on the log, with the Henry rifle propped up beside him. He listened closely, and it wasn't long until deep, regular breathing from both Elizabeth and Andrew told him that they were asleep.

He looked up but couldn't see the stars because of the pine branches overhead. The air was crisp and cool and filled with the sweet, distinctive scent of the trees. Fargo was glad to be where he was at this moment.

True, there might be trouble dogging his trail, but to a certain extent that was the case with just about everybody, no matter who or where they were. A fella just had to learn how to appreciate the moment.

Skye Fargo appreciated life, its good and bad, and intended to keep on doing so as long as he drew breath.

Especially when the air he was breathing smelled as good as it did on a spring night in the high country. . . .

Fargo dozed off a few times during the night, but never slept soundly or for long. He was still tired when dawn began to gray the sky to the east, but there would be time to sleep when they reached the trading post. He roused Elizabeth and Andrew and tried not to think how good a cup of coffee would taste right about then.

They made a quick breakfast on the last of the jerky and were riding before the sun came up. The climb to the pass was a steep one, but the horses were well rested enough to handle it. When they reached the pass, the wind that blew through was downright cold at that altitude. But this was the easiest way across the mountains and Fargo was thankful for it. As they started down the far side, the Gallatin River Valley lay before them, still shrouded in shadow because the sun wasn't yet high enough for its rays to reach over the mountains.

The sun continued its climb into the heavens, and after a while its reddish-orange glow began to penetrate into the valley. The sky overhead turned from black to gray to blue. It looked like it was going to be another beautiful day in the high country.

After handing over the Henry rifle to Elizabeth again so they would have some protection in case they ran into trouble, Fargo sent her and Andrew on ahead and lingered behind to watch the pass. If anyone came through, they would be highlighted against the glow of the sun that now filled the notch in the mountains. Fargo waited for about an hour and didn't see any signs of pursuit. He began to hope that maybe Prescott and the others hadn't come after them.

Since quite a few travelers had come that way over the years, there was a decent trail from the pass to the trading post. Fargo had no trouble following it as he rode after Elizabeth and Andrew. He thought that he would probably catch up to them by the middle of the day.

Sure enough, he came in sight of them before the sun was directly overhead. When he rode up to join them, they were bickering again. Somehow, that didn't come as a surprise to Fargo.

Elizabeth said, "I've been trying to explain to Andrew that if he wants to know more about the ways of the Bannock tribe, he should talk to you, Skye. You seem to be familiar with them."

"You expect me to ask a white man about how to be an Indian?" Andrew said.

"Skye probably knows more about it than you do," she returned tartly.

"Settle down, you two," Fargo said, feeling like a parent saddled with a couple of unruly kids. "Andrew, it's true that I've visited several Bannock villages. They're a good-hearted people who really enjoy hunting and fishing. And I never saw anybody better at making baskets."

Andrew snorted contemptuously. "Basket makers are not warriors."

"Now that's where you're wrong," Fargo said emphatically. "It's true that the Bannocks have usually been friendly to the white men, going back to the first trappers who came through this country, like Jim

Bridger and Jim Beckwourth. The Bannocks, the Shoshone, and the Paiutes are all sort of related, and they get along well with each other and with the whites. But they've fought their share of battles, too, against the Crow and the Blackfoot and other warlike tribes. Always held their own against them, too."

"Have you ever fought against them, Fargo?" Andrew wanted to know.

"As a matter of fact, I have, a time or two, when some of the bands got stirred up and went renegade."

"So you may have killed some of our relatives." There was a tone of accusation in Andrew's voice.

"Whenever I'm attacked, I defend myself," Fargo said flatly. "I make no apologies for that. But I don't go out of my way to look for trouble, and I'm always willing to live and let live. That's just the way I am."

"And Andrew should realize that," Elizabeth said. "He saw for himself how you helped him, Skye. He should be grateful."

"I didn't take a hand in this game to get thanked," Fargo said with a shrug. "I just figured it was the right thing to do."

"The noble white man," Andrew said with a sneer.

"Sort of like the noble red man that folks back east write and talk about."

Andrew glanced over at him. "They do?"

Fargo nodded and said with a friendly grin, "You should read a book called *The Last of the Mohicans*, by a fella named Cooper. He may not know a lot about actually living in the woods, but he spins a pretty good yarn and some of his Indian characters are about as noble as you'll ever find. There's a father and son named Chingachgook and Uncas, from a tribe called the Mohicans, who pretty much save the day for these white folks who keep getting in trouble. Only one who seems to know anything is a scout called

Hawkeye, and even he finds himself beset by redcoats and hostile Indians most of the time."

"What happens to the Indians?" Andrew asked. "To Uncas and Chingachgook?"

"You'll have to read the book," Fargo told him.

"I will do that," Andrew declared. "Father taught us to read English, but he has only the Bible to read."

"The Bible's a mighty fine thing to study on," Fargo said with a nod, "but folks need a good yarn sometimes, too."

They rode on, the literary discussion having mollified Andrew somewhat. He was a smart youngster, thought Fargo, but he had a prickly nature. Given the chance, he might outgrow that.

Hunger began to gnaw at their bellies. Fargo didn't want to risk a rifle shot because their enemies might still be somewhere behind them. But while they stopped to rest the horses, he managed to bring down a hare with a quick toss of the Arkansas toothpick. He skinned and cleaned the rabbit, then built a small, almost smokeless fire, and roasted the meat. It made a satisfying meal for the three of them.

They rode on, stopping only occasionally to let the horses blow. Overall, Fargo kept up a brisk pace toward the river. Come summer, this valley would be waist high with thick grass, but now the going was easy.

They reached the Gallatin in late afternoon. Fargo reined in on the bank of the swift-flowing river and pointed across to the sturdy log cabin on the opposite bank. A thin plume of smoke rose from a stone chimney at one end of the structure.

"I reckon that's the trading post?" he asked Elizabeth and Andrew.

"That's it!" Elizabeth said excitedly as she leaned forward in her saddle. "That's our home."

Andrew wasn't nearly as enthusiastic. He just nodded.

The trading post was a good-sized building with a porch that ran around three sides of it and a chimney at each end. A large tan dog stood on the porch and barked at the three riders.

In addition, there was another, windowless building off to the side, which Fargo figured was a storage shed for the pelts that Angus McAllister took in trade. A third, smaller structure, also without any windows, seemed to be a smokehouse, from the look of it. There was also a large pole corral and a shed for horses.

McAllister had built a ferry here so that travelers could cross the Gallatin River and reach his establishment without too much trouble. A heavy rope-and-pulley arrangement ran between trees on the opposite banks, with a large raft attached to it. The raft was drawn up onto the bank on the eastern side of the river, ready to carry Fargo and his companions across.

As they rode over to the raft, the door of the trading post opened and a man stepped out to see what the dog was raising a ruckus about. Even over the sound of the river, Fargo heard him exclaim, "Praise th' Lord! Andrew! Elizabeth!"

That would be Angus McAllister, thought Fargo. The Scotsman was tall and spare, with a shock of graying hair that had once been red, and a bristling beard of the same shade. He waved his arms over his head, and Elizabeth waved back. Andrew didn't, however. The youngster was stubbornly surly and not happy to be back home.

Fargo dismounted and pushed the raft off the bank onto the edge of the river. He then led the Ovaro onto the makeshift ferry. The stallion went without hesitation, completely trusting Fargo. Elizabeth and Andrew followed with their horses.

"Elizabeth, you hold the horses," Fargo said. "Andrew, give me a hand with the rope."

Together, they grasped the rope and began to pull. The current caught the raft and tried to push it downriver, but the rope was sturdy and held with no trouble. It was a hard pull. Fargo and Andrew had to struggle against the strength of the river, but eventually they brought the big raft to the other bank.

McAllister had run down to meet them. He swept Elizabeth into his arms as she stepped off the raft. "My girl!" McAllister enthused. "I was afraid I'd never see ye again!"

"I left you a note explaining what I was doing and where I'd gone," she said, a little breathless from her adoptive father's hug.

"Aye, but I feared somethin' would happen to ye. 'Tis a hard, cruel world out there, lass."

"I know," Elizabeth said. "And I might not have gotten back safely if it hadn't been for Skye here."

McAllister turned to Fargo and stuck out his big, callused hand. "Angus McAllister, at your service, lad. And ye would be . . . ?"

"Skye Fargo." He shook hands with the trader.

McAllister's pale gray eyes widened. "Th' Trailsman, as I live an' breathe! I've heard o' ye, laddie. If I'd ken that these wayward children o' mine were wi' ye, I wouldna ha' worried so much."

After pumping Fargo's hand enthusiastically, McAllister turned toward his adopted son. His grin disappeared, only to be replaced by a dark, thunderous scowl.

"And as for ye, ye ungrateful, unrepentant scalawag—"

"I only came back because Elizabeth forced me to,"

Andrew said with a scowl of his own. "I want to go to the plains and hunt a buffalo."

"Aye, I've heard aplenty about this buffalo ye're wantin' to hunt. We'll have a long talk later about what ye've done, lad, and then ye will spend some time on yer knees beggin' th' good Lord's forgiveness for all th' worry ye put yer poor old father through."

"You're not my father," Andrew snapped. "My father was a Bannock chief!"

McAllister took a deep breath. "We'll talk later," he said again, and then he turned back toward Fargo. "An' ye, Mr. Fargo, ye'll be stayin' with us for a spell?"

Fargo nodded. "If that's all right with you." He didn't think it would be a good idea for him to leave until he was confident that Prescott and the others wouldn't trail them here and show up looking for revenge.

"Ye're welcome to stay as long as ye like," McAllister said. "Our home is yer home."

He, Elizabeth, and Andrew went into the trading post while Fargo put the horses in the corral. He unsaddled the Ovaro and Elizabeth's mount, but all he had to do with Andrew's pony was remove the hackamore and the saddle pad. Then he rubbed the horses down after the long ride and made sure they had water and grain.

Fargo was sure that McAllister would have made Andrew help him with these chores if he had asked. But Fargo was just as glad for the excuse not to be present while the McAllister family hashed out their problems. He could hear the occasional raised voices from inside the trading post.

As he put the saddles on the top rail of the corral, he thought again that it might have been better for Andrew and Elizabeth if the McAllisters had let them go back to their tribe after they'd nursed them through the fever that had claimed the other members of their band. They might have had a harder time of it, but they might have been happier. At least, Andrew may have. Elizabeth didn't seem as bothered being the product of two worlds. Evidently, she had the ability to try to make the best of a situation. Not everyone was blessed with that skill.

As the light of day faded, Fargo leaned on the top rail of the fence and looked across the river toward the mountains he and his two companions had crossed earlier in the day. He couldn't help but wonder if somewhere between here and those peaks a group of hard-faced gunmen rode, eager to take vengeance on the man who had forced them to back down.

Elizabeth came out of the trading post and walked over to the corral. "Come inside, Skye," she said. "Supper is ready."

"And I'm ready for it," Fargo said with a smile.

Evidently, McAllister and Andrew had settled things, or at least had called a truce. The atmosphere around the rough-hewn table wasn't too strained. The table sat at one end of a big room mostly filled with trade goods. It was next to one of the fireplaces, where a black iron pot of stew simmered. The aroma made Fargo's mouth water.

The stew tasted as good as it smelled, and the coffee was strong and bracing. Fargo was tired after not getting much sleep the night before and the long ride. His weariness grew stronger as his belly became pleasantly full. He was looking forward to a good night's sleep.

"Ye'll have my room tonight, Mr. Fargo," McAllister said, waving a hand toward the living quarters in the back of the trading post. " 'Tis a good soft bed ye'll find there."

"I don't want to put you out of your bed," Fargo said. "I can spread my blankets in here, or out in the horse shed."

"I'll no' have ye sleepin' wi' th' horses!" McAllister exclaimed.

"Actually, it might not be a bad idea. There's a chance those men who attacked Andrew will try to follow us. If I'm outside, they won't be able to sneak up on the place as easily."

"Th' dog will alert us if anyone comes skulkin' around," McAllister insisted.

"So will my horse, if I'm out in the shed," Fargo countered.

McAllister shook his head and shrugged. "I'll no' argue wi' a guest. There's hay in th' shed, an' 'twill make a soft bed if ye spread yer blankets on it. At this time o' year, ye should be warm enough."

"That's what I thought," Fargo agreed with a smile.

McAllister looked at Andrew and went on. "Th' lad told me about his misadventures. Do ye ken why those men jumped him like that, Mr. Fargo?"

It was Fargo's turn to shake his head. "Not really, not unless it was just sheer meanness on their part. Where human beings are concerned, you can never completely discount that possibility."

"Aye, more's th' pity."

By the time they finished the meal, it was full dark outside and Fargo was ready to turn in. He said his good nights to the McAllisters, then went outside to spread his bedroll in the shed.

The evening was quiet and peaceful, and the air was already turning noticeably cooler now that the sun was gone. A million stars glittered overhead. Fargo checked on the horses, and spent a few minutes talking softly to the Ovaro and stroking the stallion's neck. Then he curled up in his blankets on a pile of hay.

One of the blankets, the one Elizabeth had used the night before, still smelled faintly of her scent. Fargo smiled as he realized that, and he was asleep mere seconds later.

He had the true frontiersman's ability to fall quickly into a sound sleep and also to wake up instantly, fully alert. When that happened sometime later, he had no idea how long he had been asleep. All he knew for sure was that the Ovaro was shifting around nearby, obviously disturbed by something. Fargo had coiled up his gun belt and placed it close beside his head. Now his hand reached out and closed around the walnut grips of the Colt.

He lay still under the shed's overhang. The stars were blocked from his view, but they cast enough light that he was able to see the figure silhouetted against the faint glow as it crept toward him. Fargo couldn't tell who it was, so he let the skulker get closer before he exploded into action.

Surging up out of the blankets, Fargo lunged forward and tackled the lurker. With a startled cry, the intruder went over backward. Fargo landed on top of the struggling figure.

That cry, along with the soft warmth underneath him, told Fargo the identity of the person he had just tackled. "Elizabeth!" he exclaimed. "What the devil are you doing out here?"

"What are *you* doing, Skye?" she demanded in turn as she ceased her struggle. "Jumping on me like I was some sort of . . . of . . . I don't know what!"

"Bushwhacker?" Fargo suggested dryly. He was well aware of how his weight flattened Elizabeth's full breasts against his chest. "Dry-gulcher?"

"You know I would never hurt you!"

"Yeah, but I didn't know who you were until I tackled you. Sneaking up on a man is a good way to get yourself hurt when you're west of the Mississippi. Probably east of there, too."

"Well, you know who I am now," she pointed out. "You could get off me."

"I could," Fargo agreed. "Or I could do this."

He let instinct guide him and brought his mouth down on hers.

He wasn't an arrogant man, but he was pretty sure he knew why she had come out here. If he was wrong, she would set him straight in a hurry. Evidently, he wasn't wrong, though, because she returned his kiss with a desperate fervor.

She reached up and put her arms around his neck, pulling him down even tighter on top of her. Fargo rolled over, keeping them locked together in each other's embrace, so that they wound up on top of his blankets. Elizabeth was still underneath him.

She wore a wool sleeping gown. When Fargo lifted his weight off her for a moment, she pulled the gown up and spread her legs wide. He pushed down his own trousers and long underwear and moved easily between her thighs. His shaft was already erect, standing out long and thick from his groin.

He touched her with his hand and found that she was ready, too. Her femininity was wet with her juices and the folds had opened like the petals of a flower. Fargo slipped a finger inside her. The intimate caress made her hips jerk a little.

Fargo worked the finger back and forth, teasing her. After a moment, she gasped, "Now, Skye, take me now! I have to have you in me!"

Fargo withdrew his finger, moved closer to her, and brought the head of his organ to her opening. He let it rest against her heated core for a second. She launched her hips upward, trying to engulf him. Slowly, Fargo penetrated her, sliding forward until his entire shaft was sheathed deep within her.

Elizabeth sighed in satisfaction. Fargo stayed where he was, filling her to the utmost. Then, after a long moment, he withdrew slightly and surged forward again. In and out, the strokes gradually lengthening, he rode her passionately.

She wrapped her legs around his hips and met his thrusts with surges of her own. They meshed perfectly in a heated, intimate dance, a coupling that lifted them higher and higher toward the peak they both sought.

But even as he was making love to her, a small part of Fargo's brain remained alert. Such unceasing vigilance was one reason he had lived as long as he had.

That, and the sheer joy he took from moments such as this one . . .

Finally, his climax shook him, and he gripped Elizabeth tightly and drove into her with one final thrust as he began to empty himself. She spasmed as well, crying out quietly. Wrapped together on the blankets, they lay there still joined, basking in the afterglow of their lovemaking.

"Your pa would probably break out his shotgun if he knew about this," Fargo whispered after several minutes.

"I may have been raised in many ways as a white girl, but I still have the hot blood of the women of my true people," she said as she snuggled against him. "I cannot fight that . . . any more than Andrew can deny his wish to hunt the buffalo."

"We'll worry about Andrew another time," Fargo said as he stroked her midnight black hair. "I reckon it's still a good while until dawn. You won't have to slip back to the trading post just yet."

"No," she agreed as her hips began to move again. "We still have plenty of time to be together." She hesitated in what she was doing and added, "But, Skye . . . don't you need some sleep? I worried about even coming out here and bothering you."

"Some sleep wouldn't hurt." Fargo chuckled softly. "But the only way you're bothering me is in a good way. To tell you the truth, what we're doing is downright invigorating, too."

5

They dozed some in each other's arms, then woke up and made love again. Finally, when the false dawn crept across the sky, Elizabeth left the shed and went back into the trading post.

Fargo hoped that Angus McAllister wouldn't catch her slipping into her room and figure out where she had been. He felt no shame at what they had done, Elizabeth was a grown woman, after all. But he didn't want to anger or embarrass McAllister, for whom he felt a genuine liking.

If McAllister had any inkling of what was going on, he gave no sign of it at breakfast, which was just as delicious as supper had been the night before. Once Fargo had eaten a couple of stacks of flapjacks and downed three cups of coffee, he felt fully human again, ready to meet whatever life had in store for him.

When he went out to check on the Ovaro after breakfast, Elizabeth followed, a worried look on her face. "Skye, are you going to be riding on today?" she asked.

He glanced toward the Bozeman Pass before he shook his head and said, "No. As long as I haven't worn out my welcome, I thought I'd stay around here for a few days."

"You still think those men will show up."

"I'm not confident they won't," Fargo said.

Elizabeth hugged herself and gave a little shiver. "When I think of what they did to Andrew, and what those other two wanted to do to me . . . it just doesn't seem right that such things could happen up here, where I've always lived."

She was right, thought Fargo. Some sort of evil was loose in the mountains. As long as it might threaten Elizabeth and her father and brother, he wanted to be close at hand to deal with it.

Andrew and Angus still seemed to have a truce. Andrew even did some chores around the trading post that morning. He was outside working some fresh chinking into the gaps between the logs on one end of the building when he called out, "Riders are coming!"

Fargo was sitting on the front porch with McAllister when they heard Andrew's shout. Elizabeth was inside. Fargo straightened up in the cane-bottomed chair he'd been leaning back against the wall. So did McAllister. Both men stood and McAllister reached for a shotgun that was leaning nearby against the wall. He tucked the double-barreled weapon under his arm as he and Fargo stepped over to the end of the porch.

They looked south along the river and saw about a dozen men on horseback approaching the trading post at a leisurely pace. They all wore buckskins and a couple of them sported feathered headdresses. Their mounts were Indian ponies, slightly smaller than normal horses. Some of the ponies were splotched with color. A few of the men carried lances; others had bows and quivers of arrows slung over their shoulders; and a few carried rifles with the barrels pointing skyward and the butts resting on their thighs.

McAllister grunted in recognition. "Three-legged Elk and some of his band," he said. "Shoshone. They're friendly."

Fargo nodded and said, "I know. Unless something happens to rile them up."

"Aye, there is that," McAllister admitted with a grin. He stepped to the edge of the porch and waved a hand over his head in greeting.

The Indians rode up to the porch and stopped. They looked awfully solemn, thought Fargo, and he wondered if something was wrong.

The leader of the group was an elderly but still powerfully built warrior with a deeply lined face the color of old mahogany. He carried a rifle and wore a bigger headdress than any of the others. He spoke to McAllister in the Shoshone tongue, the words tumbling rapidly out of his mouth.

McAllister nodded and replied in the same language. As a man who had lived among the tribes for more than two decades, he was fluent in all the languages and dialects spoken in the high country. Fargo was able to follow some of the conversation, although parts of it were a little too fast for him.

After a couple of minutes, McAllister turned to him and said, "Three-legged Elk says that there are white men on this side o' the river, comin' this way."

Fargo nodded. "I picked up that much. Does he know how many there are?"

There was another exchange of rapid-fire dialogue. McAllister said, "The Shoshones who saw these white men were out huntin'. They didna get too close. But they estimated four hands full."

Twenty men, thought Fargo. That was an even larger

bunch than he had thought might be traveling through the mountains. Large enough to be mighty dangerous if they wanted to make trouble.

"How did they get across the river?"

"There's a ford about twenty miles south o' here. They would ha' needed a ford, since they're travelin' with wagons that would ha' swamped my ferry."

"Wagons," Fargo repeated. "Covered wagons?"

McAllister passed the question along to Three-legged Elk. When the Shoshone chief had answered, the trader turned to Fargo and said, "Not prairie schooners. Smaller wagons, wi' cages on the back."

Fargo frowned. "Cages?"

"That's what Three-legged Elk said," McAllister replied with a nod.

Fargo's frown deepened as he tugged on his earlobe in thought. He couldn't figure out what this news meant.

But if the group of men with their odd wagons kept coming up the river, they would arrive at the trading post sooner or later. Fargo would have his answer then . . . but he might not like it.

"Ask him about these men," he said. Then he quickly gave McAllister verbal sketches of Prescott, Baird, Barnett, and the fourth man who had captured Andrew. He added descriptions of Devlin and the other man who had chased Elizabeth into his camp. McAllister nodded and turned to Three-legged Elk, repeating in the Shoshone language what Fargo had told him.

That took a while, since the Indian tongue was more flowery and required more words. Three-legged Elk listened intently to the question and then replied, also at length.

"Three-legged Elk says his warriors didna get close enough to th' men to tell if any o' them were th' ones ye describe, Mr. Fargo," McAllister translated. He pulled on his beard. "But I'm thinkin' those men must ha' some connection to th' ones headed here."

"I agree," Fargo said without hesitation. "I'll be very surprised if they're not all the same bunch."

Elizabeth had come up behind them on the porch and listened to the discussion. Now she said, "That means we've got trouble on the way, doesn't it?"

From the ground, Andrew said, "I hope those men *are* with them. I want a chance to settle the score." He lifted a hand and gingerly touched his forehead, which still had a bandage wrapped around it.

That was the folly of youth speaking, thought Fargo. It wouldn't be so easy settling "the score," as Andrew put it. Not against odds of five to one.

Unless . . .

He said to McAllister, "Is there any chance Three-legged Elk and his warriors would stay here and help us deal with these men if they attack?"

McAllister drew himself up straight without passing along the question. "I wouldna ask such a thing of a friend," he declared. "If there is to be trouble, 'twould be none o' th' Shoshones' affair. Th' McAllisters fight their own battles, laddie."

Fargo grinned and squeezed the trader's arm. "That's pretty much what I thought you'd say, Angus, but I felt like I had to suggest it."

Three-legged Elk spoke again. McAllister translated. "They warned us out o' friendship, but now they will be returnin' to their village." He faced the chief, clenched his right hand into a fist, and lightly tapped his chest. "Farewell, my friend."

"Farewell, McAllister," Three-legged Elk replied in English, his tongue wrapping itself thickly around the words.

The Indians turned and rode away, disappearing a

few minutes later in the trees along the river. Elizabeth put a hand on McAllister's shoulder and asked worriedly, "What are we going to do, Father?"

"For one thing, we'll not borrow trouble," replied McAllister. " 'Tis possible these men mean us no harm. They may no' even belong to th' same bunch that plagued ye an' yer brother."

Fargo thought that was pretty unlikely, but he didn't contradict McAllister.

The trader turned to him and said, "Will ye be ridin' on now, Mr. Fargo?"

With a faint smile, Fargo said, "We haven't known each other for very long, Angus, but even so, *you* ought to know better than to ask *that*."

McAllister threw back his head and laughed. "Aye, so I should!" He grew more sober as he went on. "We'd best be about gettin' ready. Company's comin' to call."

And it was likely, Fargo thought, that the visit wasn't going to be very pleasant.

By the time the group of riders and wagons came into sight, traveling slowly along the river toward the trading post, Fargo and the McAllisters had prepared for trouble as best they could. The four of them were inside, behind the sturdy log walls of the trading post, and all the guns they had were loaded and ready. The shutters were drawn closed over all the windows except one, and those were ready to be shut tight, with only a narrow gap remaining between them.

That window was where Fargo stood, watching through the gap as the strangers approached. He lifted a spyglass to his eye and squinted through the lens. The driver of the lead wagon leaped into sharp focus.

Fargo had never seen the man before. He handled the reins well, but he was obviously more than just a teamster. He wore a six-gun on his hip and had a rifle on the seat next to him. His features had the same arrangement of hard planes and angles that Fargo had seen on the other men with whom he'd had trouble in recent days.

Shifting the glass to one of the men riding on horseback next to the wagon, Fargo stiffened as he recognized the man called Baird. That pretty much settled the question of whether or not Andrew's kidnappers had come from this group. Fargo then checked the other men as well and spotted Prescott, Barnett, and the other man, whose name he didn't know, all of them riding alongside the wagons.

Then he focused on the other drivers. There were six wagons in all, and on one of them was a man with his right arm in a sling who rode beside the driver. Fargo recognized the long hair and the narrow, predatory face. That was the man who had been with Devlin, the one whose shoulder Fargo had broken with a well-placed shot.

All the chickens were coming home to roost, thought Fargo as he lowered the spyglass for a moment. Then he raised it again and studied the wagons themselves.

They were big, sturdy vehicles, each pulled by a team of six large, strong mules. As Three-legged Elk had reported, each wagon had a cage on the back, with walls made of wooden slats set a couple of inches apart. They might have been divided up into smaller sections inside. Fargo couldn't tell. But he was sure that some of the cages had occupants. He could see movement through the gaps between the slats, but he couldn't make out what was penned up in the cages.

Finally, bringing up the rear of the little caravan was a closed coach drawn by a four-horse hitch. Another hardcase sat on the high box, holding the reins. The coach was probably carrying passengers, but Fargo had no idea who they could be.

He went back to looking at the outriders, and two of them didn't fit in, he realized. They were older and more grizzled, and they wore buckskins. One of them had on an old felt hat with a round crown and a wide brim; the other wore a coonskin cap with the tail of the raccoon still attached and pulled around so that it rested on his right shoulder. Both men looked vaguely familiar to Fargo, but he couldn't place them.

"All right," Fargo said to the McAllisters as he closed up the spyglass and set it on a shelf next to the window. "The men who grabbed Andrew are out there, and so is the one I shot a couple of days ago."

"Then we know they're here to attack us," Andrew said. "We should open fire on them while they're not expecting anything."

"Such treachery is unbecomin', lad," McAllister growled, "an' I hate to hear such a suggestion comin' from somebody I raised."

"But they're evil!" Andrew protested. "You didn't see them, Pa."

Elizabeth said, "Andrew is right, Pa. We shouldn't take chances."

McAllister was steadfast. "We'll no' be turnin' into bushwhackers," he declared.

Fargo agreed with him. Strategically, it might be better to whittle down the odds while they had the chance. But they didn't *know* that the men intended to make trouble again. For men such as Skye Fargo and Angus McAllister, strategy sometimes had to take a backseat to honor.

The lead wagon and the first outriders were only about fifty yards away now. Fargo said, "Stay in here and keep your guns ready. I'll go out and talk to them."

"Skye"—Elizabeth's voice was anxious—"be careful."

"I intend to be," Fargo assured her.

He picked up his Henry and went to the front door. He opened it just enough so that he could slip out, and then quickly closed it behind him. He stepped to the edge of the porch and stood there waiting, apparently casual, but in reality poised to move fast if he had to.

Prescott and Baird spotted him and leaned forward in their saddles as if they were about to gallop the rest of the way to the trading post. But one of the old-timers in buckskin stopped them with an outstretched hand and a sharp word. The wagon drivers hauled back on their reins and brought the big vehicles to a halt. The other riders reined in as well.

That left the two buckskinners to ride forward and greet Fargo. They did so, keeping their hands well away from their guns. Fargo kept one eye on them and one eye on the other men, just in case the hotheaded Prescott made a grab for his gun while the older men's backs were turned.

Prescott behaved, though, just sitting there with a glare on his face directed toward Fargo. The buckskinners reined their mounts to a halt in front of the trading post. The man in the coonskin cap lifted a hand and said, "Howdy. Is this the McAllister place?"

"It is," Fargo said. He asked bluntly, "Who are you?"

"Jeb Tolbert," the man replied. He leaned his head toward his companion. "And this is Bart Stanton."

Tolbert was tall and lean, with gray beard stubble on his jaw. The shorter and stockier Stanton had a broad, florid face under the wide brim of his hat.

The names were familiar. Fargo nodded and said, "I've heard of both of you. Been hunting and trapping up in these mountains for quite a while, haven't you?"

Tolbert grinned. "That's a fact. I came out here in thirty-five, and Bart's first year was, what, eighteen and forty?"

Stanton nodded and said, "Yep. I got in on the last few rendezvouses before the Shinin' Times were pretty much over."

"There's still plenty of trapping going on," Fargo pointed out.

"Yeah, but it ain't like it used to be," Tolbert said. He lowered his voice a little as he added, "That's why fellas like us sometimes have to work for folks like them."

He jerked his head toward the wagons, the coach, and the other outriders.

"You look a mite familiar, mister," Stanton put in. "What's your handle?"

"Skye Fargo."

Both Stanton and Tolbert looked surprised. Clearly, the name meant something to them.

"You're the Trailsman," Tolbert said. "I heard that you cleaned up the Vaca gang down around Taos a couple of years back."

Fargo nodded. "I had a run-in with them, all right."

"Run-in, hell. You killed Esteban Vaca and busted up the rest of his bunch." Tolbert nodded. "I'm obliged to you for that, Fargo. That bastard Vaca once killed a friend of mine."

"He deserved what he got, all right," Fargo agreed.

"Where's McAllister?" Stanton asked. "We were told this was his place."

"It is." Fargo smiled grimly. "But there's been some trouble in these parts the past few days, so McAllister and a couple of other folks are inside right now with rifles pointed at the two of you, just in case."

Tolbert laughed, but there was no humor in the sound. It was more like metal filings rattling around in a bucket. "Trouble is one thing we ain't lookin' for, Fargo."

"Then you're keeping the wrong company."

Both men glanced over their shoulders at the wagons. "You might be right about that," Tolbert said. "You got to make allowances for folks who ain't never been in the high country before, though."

"I do make allowances," Fargo said. "That's why we didn't start shooting as soon as you boys got in range. Now, tell me why you're here and what you want."

Tolbert and Stanton looked more than slightly annoyed at Fargo's tone, but they didn't lose their tempers. Instead, Tolbert said, "We're on a huntin' trip. An 'expedition,' the boss calls it."

"Who's the boss?"

"Fella name of Olney. Richard Francis Olney."

Olney was the other name Andrew had overhead his captors mentioning, so it didn't come as any big surprise to Fargo. Other than that, however, the name meant nothing to him.

"And just who is Richard Francis Olney?"

Tolbert grinned. "We'd better let him tell you his ownself. He's good at that." He jerked a thumb over his shoulder at the rest of the group. "All right to go back and fetch him?"

"Go ahead," Fargo told him. "Just don't try anything funny."

"Never entered my mind," Tolbert said.

Fargo looked at Stanton. "And you stay here."

The burly mountain man shrugged. "Sure. It don't matter none to me."

Tolbert turned his horse around and trotted back to the wagons. He rode past the vehicles all the way to the coach in the rear. A door in the side of the coach opened, and Tolbert spoke to somebody inside.

From where Fargo stood on the porch, he couldn't tell anything about the occupant.

The conversation must have been satisfactory, though, because the door of the coach closed and Tolbert spoke to the driver. The man pulled the coach out of line and slapped the reins against the backs of the horses. He drove past the stopped wagons toward the trading post. Tolbert rode alongside.

When the coach reached the building, the driver brought the team to a stop and stayed where he was on the high seat. Tolbert leaned over in his saddle and opened the door. "Mr. Olney," he said, "this here is Skye Fargo."

The man who stepped out of the coach was small, no more than five-and-a-half feet tall. He carried himself like a larger man, though. He wore an expensive suit and a beaver hat that looked out of place here on the frontier. It was more the sort of getup that a man might wear back in Philadelphia or New York. His face was rounded and his clean-shaven cheeks shone. He had sleek black hair under the beaver hat.

He bounded up the steps to the porch of the trading post with a self-confidence that bordered on arrogance. Extending a small, well-manicured hand, he said, "Mr. Fargo, is it? I'm very glad to meet you. Jeb here tells me that you're quite a well-known frontiersman."

Fargo took Olney's hand. The little man's grip was surprisingly firm.

"I'm Richard Francis Olney of the Philadelphia Olneys," he went on, confirming Fargo's hunch about his origins. "Perhaps you've heard of me."

"Can't say as I have," Fargo replied dryly.

That didn't seem to bother Olney. "Oh, well, that's fine. I have something of a reputation as an amateur naturalist and natural scientist, but I suppose that only extends among certain circles back east. *I'd* never heard of *you*, either."

"I reckon we're even, then."

Olney chuckled. "Indeed." He waved a hand toward the wagons. "Did Jeb explain to you the purpose of our expedition, Mr. Fargo?"

"Not really."

"I've come out here to amass a collection of specimens of native Western animal life. I'm in the process of establishing a private museum and wildlife exhibition park back in Philadelphia."

That was the first time Fargo had ever heard of such a thing, but as he thought about it, he understood what Olney was talking about. As he had hinted at during his conversation with Andrew about James Fenimore Cooper's novel, folks back east had a fascination with life on the frontier. He supposed it was a way of getting some of the excitement of living in the West without having to face all the dangers that went with it. Nothing was wrong with that, as far as Fargo was concerned, although he knew that he would have been stifled half to death if he had to live back there in civilization.

He nodded toward the wagons and said, "So you hired a couple of experienced trappers and hunters to catch some wild animals for you, and you've got the beasts caged up in those wagons."

"Precisely!" Olney said with a smile. "I commend you on your astuteness, Mr. Fargo. You figured that out immediately."

"It wasn't all that hard," Fargo said. "What I don't understand is why you've got a bunch of no-good skunks like those other fellas riding with you."

That blunt statement shook Olney's confident smile. "My, uh, other associates," he said, "were hired to make certain that my sister and I are protected during the expedition and remain safe until we return to Philadelphia."

"Sister?" Fargo repeated with a frown.

"That's right," a female voice said from the coach. "Honestly, Richard, I was beginning to think that you were never going to get around to mentioning me to the very handsome Mr. Fargo."

6

Fargo looked over at the coach and saw a woman in her late twenties standing in the open door. She was dressed in an expensive, dark blue traveling gown and had a feathered hat of the same shade perched on her coppery hair. She was very attractive but, like her brother, looked rather out of place here in front of a trading post on the Gallatin River.

"I'm sorry, Victoria," Olney said hastily. He hurried down the steps and over to the coach to take her hand and help her climb down to the ground, then escorted her up to the porch. "Mr. Fargo, allow me to present my sister, Mrs. Victoria Arrowsmith. Victoria, this is Mr. Skye Fargo."

As he touched a finger to the brim of his hat, Fargo murmured, "Ma'am."

"Hello, Mr. Fargo," she said. "I suppose you're wondering what a woman such as myself is doing out here in the middle of this vast wilderness."

"The thought did cross my mind," Fargo admitted.

"Why, I had to come along to look after Richard, of course. The poor dear is so devoted to his scientific endeavors that he forgets to take care of himself properly. Why, sometimes he would even forget to eat if no one reminded him. And since my late husband, Walter, passed away, I've needed something to occupy my time."

"So you're a widow, then, ma'am?" Fargo asked.

"That's right."

That explained a certain boldness in her eyes as she looked at him, he thought. It was a look of appraisal, perhaps even of hunger. He didn't much care for it.

Olney must have missed the way his sister was studying Fargo, because he went on. "You see, Mr. Fargo, my sister and I are not lacking in financial resources. Our father was involved with banking and shipbuilding and was quite successful at both. In addition, Victoria's late husband was also quite wealthy. So we have the funds to indulge in our respective passions . . . mine for scientific research and hers for travel and—"

"Excitement," Victoria finished with a smile.

Lord, Lord, thought Fargo. They were a pair, all right, and neither one of them had any real business being out here. But they were here, and they had those hardcases with them, so he would just have to deal with the situation the way it was.

"As I was saying before you introduced your sister to me, you have some men working for you who have been causing trouble around here," he said.

Olney frowned. "I'm afraid I have no idea what you're talking about, Mr. Fargo. I know nothing of this." He turned to look at Tolbert and Stanton. "Jeb, Bart, do either of you know what Mr. Fargo is talking about?"

The two mountain men looked uncomfortable. "Maybe we do, Mr. Olney," Tolbert said. "Might be better if Fargo explained to you what he means, though. We ain't heard his side of the story."

Olney looked at Fargo again. "Yes, if there's a problem, please tell me."

"All right," Fargo said. Pulling no punches, he went on. "Several days ago, a couple of your men chased and tried to attack a young woman. I stopped them. Then yesterday, four more of them were in the middle of beating a boy when I came along. They might have killed him if they'd kept it up."

Olney and his sister both stared at Fargo. After a moment, Olney said, "I assure you, Mr. Fargo, this is the first I've heard of these matters. How do you know that the men involved in these incidents belong to my party?"

"Because I can see 'em right over there," Fargo replied, with a nod toward the wagons. "Three of them are named Prescott, Baird, and Barnett. One of them whose name I don't know has his arm in a sling because I shot him in the shoulder."

"That'd be Strayhorn, Mr. Olney," Tolbert put in.

Olney looked at him again. "You say you *knew* about this, Jeb?"

Tolbert rested his hands on the cantle of his saddle and leaned forward. "Well, not exactly. I knew that Strayhorn and Devlin had run into some trouble. That Devlin got himself killed and Strayhorn took a bullet. But Strayhorn claimed they ran into some renegade Injuns who took potshots at them. He never said nothing about Mr. Fargo here."

"And the business with Prescott and the others?" Olney snapped.

"Again, they claimed they'd been jumped by Injuns and had a runnin' fight with them. This is the first I've heard about them beatin' up some kid."

Olney turned back to Fargo. "Meaning no disrespect, sir, but can you furnish any proof of these allegations you've made? It's true that regular scouting parties, including the men you mentioned, have left the expedition from time to time, but they made no reports of trouble to me."

"That's because they didn't want you to know the truth," Fargo said. He figured that with Olney and Mrs. Arrowsmith standing on the porch, it would be safe enough to bring out the McAllisters. The hardcases wouldn't be likely to open fire with their boss standing right there next to Fargo. He went to the door of the trading post, opened it, and said, "Come on out."

Angus McAllister came first, followed by Andrew and Elizabeth. Fargo was watching Prescott and Baird as the McAllister siblings stepped out where the gunmen could see them. Both of the hardcases stiffened in their saddles—Fargo could tell that even at a distance. They recognized Andrew, all right.

"Mr. Olney, this is Angus McAllister, the owner of this trading post," Fargo said. "And his children, Elizabeth and Andrew."

"Amazing," Olney muttered. "They appeared to be full-blooded Indians."

"They are," McAllister said. "But they're also me children. I've raised 'em since they were wee bairns."

"Elizabeth is the young woman who was nearly attacked by Devlin and Strayhorn," Fargo explained. "And the gash under the bandage around Andrew's head came from Prescott's gun barrel when he pistol-whipped the boy. Prescott and Baird gave him the bruises you see on his face."

Victoria Arrowsmith murmured, "Barbaric. Simply barbaric."

"I thought so, too," Fargo agreed. "That's why I put a stop to it."

Olney looked at Tolbert and Stanton. "What do the two of you think?" he demanded. "Are our men capable of the sort of behavior Mr. Fargo has described?"

For a moment, the two mountain men didn't answer. Clearly, they didn't want to be put in the middle of a bad situation like this. But finally, Tolbert said, "I've heard of Fargo. I reckon he ain't the sort of hombre who goes around makin' up stories."

"Chances are what he says is true," added Stanton.

Olney drew in a deep breath and let it out in a sigh. "Well, then," he said to Fargo, "I apologize if I appeared to doubt you, sir."

"No apology necessary," Fargo told him. "You just needed to know the truth about the men who are working for you."

"Indeed I do. There'll be no more trouble. I give you my word on that."

Fargo wasn't sure how this dandified little dilettante from back east was going to enforce that promise. He was paying Prescott and the others, but in the end that might not be enough.

Olney turned to McAllister and went on. "Mr. McAllister, back in Saint Louis where this expedition started, I was told about your trading post and given directions on how to find it. This is a game-rich area, and I'd like to make this my headquarters, so to speak, while the expedition is in the vicinity. Do I have your permission to establish a camp there by the river where my wagons are stopped?"

"Th' river don't belong to me, an' neither does th' land alongside it," McAllister said. "Make camp where'er ye like, Mr. Olney. I canna stop ye."

"But I want to be a good neighbor while I'm here," Olney said. "I'd like to be sure that our being nearby won't cause you any discomfort. Under the circumstances, I'll certainly understand if you wish for us to move on."

McAllister hesitated. He was a hospitable man by nature, Fargo thought, and yet the men who worked for Olney had caused considerable trouble for his family.

Fargo stepped into the gap. "Prescott, Baird, and the others are probably carrying considerable grudges against me," he said. "They're liable to be looking to settle the score."

"I'll issue strict orders that there is to be no trouble while we're here," Olney said. He looked at the trader. "And I can make it well worth your while, Mr. McAllister. It's quite likely we'll be needing some supplies, and you're the only source for them within a hundred miles or more."

Appealing to McAllister's business sense was a smart move, thought Fargo. Clearly, Olney had plenty of money and didn't mind spending it. McAllister looked at Elizabeth and Andrew and asked, "Wha' do th' two o' ye think?"

Andrew shrugged. "I don't care, as long as those men stay away from me."

"I feel the same way," Elizabeth said with a nod.

"All right." McAllister turned back to Olney. "I reckon 'tis all right wi' us if ye make camp here . . . if that's all right wi' Fargo."

Fargo wasn't worried about Prescott and the others. If they started any trouble, he would deal with it. Under the circumstances, he thought things had worked out better than they'd had any right to expect. Earlier, they had thought that the trading post might come under an all-out attack. The presence of Olney and Mrs. Arrowsmith had come as a distinct surprise.

"Keep your men down there by the river," he said

to Olney. He looked at Tolbert and Stanton. "I figure you men know what I'm saying."

"Aye," Tolbert said. "There'll be no trouble, Fargo."

"I guess it's settled, then," Olney said with a smile.

"You an' th' lady are welcome here," McAllister said.

Elizabeth came closer to Victoria Arrowsmith and stared at the expensive traveling outfit the older woman wore. "That's a beautiful dress," Elizabeth said.

"You speak English well," Victoria said, looking and sounding surprised.

"Yes, my mother taught me to read and write her language. As Father said, Andrew and I have been with them since we were children. Mother passed away a few years ago from the fever. She never wore a dress such as this, though." Elizabeth reached out tentatively. "Do you mind if I . . . touch the fabric?"

"Go ahead, dear," Victoria said with an indulgent smile. "I have a feeling you and I are going to be good friends."

Andrew wasn't interested in being friends with the visitors. With a grunt, he turned and went into the trading post.

"I'll go back and explain the situation to the men," Olney said. "Victoria, are you staying here?"

"Yes, go ahead, Richard. I'll stay here with my new friend Elizabeth."

"Will you tell me all about Philadelphia?" Elizabeth asked as she and Victoria strolled along the porch.

"Of course, dear."

Olney climbed back in the coach, and the driver turned it around and headed back to rejoin the rest of the expedition.

Stanton said to Tolbert, "I'll go along and see about gettin' camp set up."

Tolbert nodded. He waited until Stanton had ridden off, then he dismounted and stepped up onto the porch, taking out a pipe and a pouch of tobacco.

"Hope you got some 'baccy," he said to McAllister. "I'm startin' to run a mite low."

"Aye, we can accommodate ye on that," McAllister assured him.

Tolbert got his pipe filled and lit. When it was drawing well, he said to Fargo, "I had a hunch Strayhorn wasn't tellin' the whole story about what happened to him and Devlin. Same thing with Prescott and his friends. Out here, it's easy to blame ever'thing on Injuns, but it ain't always true."

"Where did Olney come up with that bunch, anyway?" asked Fargo.

"He hired 'em in Saint Louis. Put an ad in the paper lookin' for drivers and guards. What he got was a bunch o' hardcases and borderline owlhoots." Tolbert shrugged. "But I got to admit, they've behaved themselves so far. Around the wagons, anyway. From what you've told us, they got up to plenty of mischief whilst they was out scoutin'."

"They sure did," Fargo agreed grimly. "Do you think they'll do what Olney tells them to do and steer clear of the trading post?"

Tolbert thought it over before answering. "Olney's promised them all more money when this expedition of his gets back to Saint Louis. There's a chance that'll be enough to make them go along with him." He added, "But I'd keep my eyes open anyway."

"I intend to," Fargo said.

By evening, the camp down by the river seemed to be well established. The wagons had been pulled into a rough circle, and the mule teams were unhitched and picketed out to graze, as were the saddle horses.

The men had a fire going and were getting ready to cook supper. None had come anywhere near the trading post. Fargo knew that because he had been watching them all afternoon.

Richard Olney had come back to the post, though, and spent quite a bit of time talking to McAllister about the animal life in the area. It was clear that Olney considered the trader to be an expert on that subject, and McAllister enjoyed the discussion.

Elizabeth spent the day asking Victoria Arrowsmith all the questions she could think of about life back in Philadelphia. Elizabeth was fascinated by the older woman. Victoria seemed flattered by the attention, although it took her a while to become accustomed to having such a conversation with a young woman who, in Victoria's eyes, was little more than a savage.

Jeb Tolbert talked quite a bit with Fargo. As it turned out, they had been to many of the same places and knew many of the same people. The frontier, for all its vast, wide-open expanses, was really a small place in many ways.

Tolbert also talked about the animals that the expedition had caught during the journey out here. Trapping an animal for its pelt was one thing. In that case, it didn't matter if the animal wound up dead. But Olney wanted his specimens alive, which meant rigging snares and setting traps that used nets and ropes to capture the animals without hurting them. They couldn't be used for Olney's planned wildlife exhibition park if they were dead.

"He calls it a zool . . . 'zoological garden,' " Tolbert explained, hesitating over the unfamiliar word. "I never heard of such a thing myself, but he says there was a Philadelphia Zoological Society or some such started last year."

"I've heard of parks like that," Fargo said. "The

ancient Greeks and Romans had them, and I think the old Chinese and Egyptians did, too. There are some over in Europe now, in places like Spain and Prussia. I read about 'em in an old newspaper."

"Seems strange to me, havin' a place where folks can come and look at animals." Tolbert waved a hand at the mountains. "Out here you can see all the animals you'd ever want just by lookin' around."

"Back east, things aren't like they are out here," Fargo reminded him.

Tolbert snorted. "Ain't that the blessed truth! That's why I don't intend to ever set foot east of the Mississippi again."

Late in the afternoon, Olney sought out Fargo and found the Trailsman sitting on the porch with Tolbert. The Easterner said, "Mr. Fargo, according to Mr. McAllister, you're very well-known as a guide and frontiersman. I was wondering if you'd be interested in working for me while I'm out here."

Fargo inclined his head toward Tolbert. "You've got Jeb here and Bart Stanton to serve as guides and supervise the trapping of the animals you're after. You don't need me."

"On the contrary," Olney said. "One can face an infinite variety of challenges in the wilderness, and the more experienced allies one has, the better one's chances of success. Wouldn't you say that's true, Mr. Fargo?"

"It might be," Fargo admitted.

"And haven't you worked as a guide for parties from back east before?"

"I have," Fargo said.

"Unless, of course, you're committed to some other employment of which I'm not aware . . . ?"

Seeing that Olney was going to be persistent, Fargo

said, "I'll think about it. That's all I can say right now."

"Excellent! I appreciate your consideration, Mr. Fargo. I promise you, if you become one of my associates, I'll make it well worth your while."

"We'll see," Fargo said.

A short time later, Angus McAllister again offered to let Olney and Mrs. Arrowsmith stay at the trading post, but Olney assured him that wouldn't be necessary.

"The coach is equipped with special seats that fold down to become a bed," he explained. "My sister stays in there. I have a fine tent of my own, and my men should have it set up by now."

Elizabeth said, "Oh, but you'll stay for supper, at least, won't you, Mrs. Arrowsmith? And you, too, of course, Mr. Olney?"

"Well, I don't know," Victoria said. "What do you think, Richard?"

"Who could turn down such a charming invitation?" Olney said with a smile. "Of course, we'll stay, my dear."

"I'll get everything ready," Elizabeth enthused.

Meanwhile, her brother sat sullenly in a corner of the big room. Andrew wanted to embrace the Indian side of his heritage, but it had become obvious over the course of the afternoon that Elizabeth was much more fascinated by Mrs. Arrowsmith. She would have been perfectly happy to go back east with the expedition and see for herself just how the whites lived. Fargo figured she wouldn't mind giving that way of life a try for herself.

He had a feeling that if she ever did go east, though, she would wind up missing her father and her brother, not to mention the land itself: the majestic mountains, the sweeping plains, the big blue sky that arched overhead like the very dome of Heaven itself. Those things got in a person's blood. Once somebody had spent some time out here, it was rare that they could go back to any other place and be happy. Fargo was sure it happened that way sometimes, of course . . . but he couldn't understand it and never would.

They had elk steaks for supper, cooked with wild onions. Fargo thought the meal was quite good, but though Olney and Victoria didn't complain, he could tell that they had trouble chewing the tough meat. Elizabeth dished out some wild berries to finish off the meal.

When they were done, Olney and McAllister brought out pipes and sat at the table, continuing their discussion of the area's wildlife. Andrew built up the fire in the fireplace and sat down cross-legged before it. Elizabeth would have been happy to continue talking to Victoria, but the older woman shook her head and smiled.

"I'm really quite tired, dear," she said. "I believe I'll go back to the coach and retire for the evening. I'm sure you understand."

"Oh." Elizabeth looked and sounded disappointed, but after a moment she put up a good front. "Of course. Thank you for telling me about Philadelphia, Mrs. Arrowsmith. I've never heard anything more interesting."

"Well, it helps to have a receptive audience," Victoria said, still smiling. She turned toward Fargo and surprised him a little by sliding her arm through his, linking them at the elbows. "Would you be so kind as to escort me back to the coach, Mr. Fargo? The sun has set, and I don't like walking through the wilderness at night by myself."

Fargo's surprise didn't last long. He recalled how she had looked at him earlier, and he knew she was just angling for some time alone with him. On the other hand, she really was right about wanting someone to walk with her back to the expedition's camp. Chances were, he wouldn't have let her leave the trading post by herself anyway.

"All right, Mrs. Arrowsmith," he said. "I'll see you safely home, so to speak."

"You're quite the gentleman, not at all like so many of the ruffians we've encountered out here. Thank you."

Arm in arm, Fargo and Victoria started for the door. A glance over his shoulder told Fargo that Elizabeth was glaring after them, clearly displeased by this turn of events.

But just who exactly was she jealous of? he asked himself. Given the way Elizabeth had pestered Victoria all afternoon, he wasn't sure of the answer.

They left the trading post and started toward the camp. With the sun gone, the air had quickly lost any warmth it had gained from the day. A cold breeze blew in their faces.

Fargo felt a shiver go through Victoria. "It's spring," she said. "Shouldn't the nights be warmer than this?"

"We're up high enough here so that the nights are hardly ever warm, no matter what time of year it is. Sometimes there's frost on the ground in the morning, even in the middle of summer."

"Well, it's certainly not like that back in Philadelphia. The summers there can be positively beastly, they're so hot and oppressive."

"You won't find that out here," Fargo said.

Victoria stopped, forcing him to halt as well since their arms were still linked. They were about halfway between the trading post and the expedition's camp.

They stood under some aspen trees whose leaves diffused the moonlight and softened its silvery glow. Victoria turned toward Fargo and said, "I found one thing out here that I never expected to."

"What's that?" asked Fargo, although he thought he might know what her answer was going to be.

"The most handsome man I've seen in a long time. I hope you don't mind if I say that you're incredibly attractive, Mr. Fargo."

"And you're a lovely woman, Mrs. Arrowsmith. Any man with eyes in his head can see that."

"You strike me as a man who truly sees where others only look," she murmured.

"I keep my eyes open," Fargo said dryly.

She moved closer to him. She wasn't wearing her hat now, and her dark red hair was loose around her head. The moonlight struck coppery glints off it. Fargo smelled the sweet, subtle scent of perfume—perfume, out here in the middle of nowhere!

"You must think me bold," she said as she rested a hand on his chest.

"I think we're right here between the trading post and the camp, where folks can see us."

"They can't see us very well under these trees," Victoria said. "We can do whatever we want, and no one will ever know." She laughed. "*Now* do you think I'm bold?"

"I don't reckon there's anything else I could think," Fargo said.

She laughed again and moved her hand from his chest to the back of his neck. She drew his face down to hers and kissed him.

She was good at it, Fargo had to give her that. Her lips were full and hot and sweet, and they parted eagerly when his tongue stroked them. Her body melded against his. His arms went around her waist and tightened. Even through their clothing, he could feel every sensuous curve of her.

Her tongue met his in a wanton duel, darting and swooping and circling. Fargo slid a hand down to her hips and caressed their rich roundness. His shaft had hardened almost instantly against the softness of her belly. She pressed herself against it and moaned deep in her throat as they kissed.

Victoria slipped a hand between them and closed it over his erection. She squeezed, sending throbs of pleasure through him. When she finally broke the kiss, she whispered, "Let me do something for you, Mr. Fargo . . . Skye."

Fargo didn't tell her no or try to stop her as she slid to her knees in front of him. With practiced ease, her fingers unfastened the buttons of his buckskin trousers and slid inside to free his manhood. The long, thick pole sprang free.

Victoria laughed. "Be careful," she said mischievously. "You could hurt a girl with that."

She wrapped both hands around his shaft and rubbed her cheek against the head. Fargo's jaw tightened as he felt the warmth of her breath on the sensitive flesh. Her tongue flicked out, striking him lightly here and there. Clearly, she was an expert at what she was doing.

After stroking and teasing him for several moments, she kissed the head of his shaft and then opened her mouth to draw it in. Her lips closed around his member and she began to suck gently. Fargo rested his hands on her head and moved his hips just a little, barely sliding back and forth in her mouth. She made another noise in her throat and sucked harder.

Fargo had as strong a will as any man west of the Mississippi, but not even he could withstand such exquisite torment for very long. He felt his climax building in a series of throbs that went through him and stiffened his shaft even more than it already was. Victoria must have sensed what was about to happen, because she took her lips away from him just long enough to gasp, "Give it to me, Skye! Give me everything!"

Then her mouth engulfed him again, the lips closing firmly around him, and her tongue slid along the underside of his organ. Fargo's culmination washed over him. He thrust into her mouth and his seed burst from him. Victoria swallowed, trying to keep up with each scalding salvo, but some escaped her mouth and ran down her chin. Her hands pulled at him, milking every possible drop.

As Fargo stood there, basking in the afterglow of what had just happened, his brain was still alert enough to realize that he hadn't meant for it to happen. He wasn't sure that getting involved with Victoria Arrowsmith was a good idea. She was vain and self-centered. Even though she had come on this expedition with her brother, Fargo was able to tell that she didn't really like the frontier. She would be glad when they got back to Philadelphia.

Of course, Fargo wasn't the sort to even think about settling down, either. At this point in his life, pleasure was still a thing of the moment . . . and any way you looked at it, the moment he had just shared with Victoria had been mighty pleasurable.

So maybe it would be all right after all, he told himself. He helped Victoria to her feet and held her with her head resting against his chest. She sighed in contentment.

"I have to get back," she said at last, "but we'll have to find the right time and place to get together again, Skye. Please, think about Richard's offer. If you were working for him and accompanied us back to Philadelphia, you and I could spend a great deal of time together."

For a second, Fargo wondered if Olney had put her up to this. Then he decided that wasn't the case. He figured Victoria was too proud to go along with such a suggestion. It was just that both she and her brother wanted Fargo to join the expedition.

He already knew that wasn't going to happen. Jeb Tolbert and Bart Stanton were good men, the sort of hombres Fargo wouldn't mind riding the river with. But as for the rest of the bunch working for Olney . . . Fargo wanted no part of them.

He didn't say anything about that, however, not wanting to anger or upset Victoria. There would be time enough later to give Olney his decision.

He kissed her on the forehead and then slid an arm around her shoulders. "Come on. Let's get you back to your coach. It's been a long day and you need to turn in and get some rest."

"Yes," she said with a light laugh. "I think I do."

They walked the rest of the way to the camp without incident. The men had built a good-sized fire. Some were still gathered around, talking and smoking. A desultory poker game went on, the cards being dealt on a blanket spread on the ground. Several of the men had already turned in and were rolled up in their bedrolls, including Tolbert and Stanton.

Fargo took Victoria to her coach and waited until she had climbed inside before leaving. She said, "Good night, Mr. Fargo," and he said, "Good night, Mrs. Arrowsmith." Neither of them gave any indication of what had passed between them under the trees.

If Tolbert and Stanton had still been awake, Fargo might have stopped and visited with them for a few minutes. But since both of the buckskinners were snoring in their blankets, he headed straight back to the trading post. He would say good night to the McAllisters, check on the Ovaro, and then turn in himself, stretching out on his makeshift bunk in the shed.

He was passing through the same grove of trees where he and Victoria had paused for their passionate interlude, when a slight noise behind him made him stop short. Instinct prompted him to begin to whirl around—

But he had made it only halfway when something exploded on the side of his head.

7

Fargo went down but not out, driven to one knee by the blow that had come out of the darkness to smash against his skull. His hat flew off his head. His grip on consciousness wavered for a second, but he recovered in time to hear the swish in the air as something came toward his head again. He threw himself forward.

The blow missed, and Fargo heard a startled grunt as he rolled over on the ground. His attacker had been thrown off balance by that miss. Fargo twisted, saw the dark shape looming above him, and his leg shot out to hook behind the man's left ankle. With a sharp tug, Fargo pulled the man's legs out from under him.

Fargo kept rolling and came up on his feet. The shadowy attacker scrambled up, too, and lunged at Fargo, slashing the club in his hand back and forth as he charged. Fargo couldn't tell for sure, but he thought the bludgeon was a broken tree branch.

Whatever it was, it had hurt like hell when it walloped him a few seconds earlier. He thought that the fact he was moving at the time was the only thing that had saved him from a shattered skull. His movement had turned a killing blow into a glancing one.

Fargo ducked another swing of the club, stepped inside, and hammered a punch to his opponent's midsection. The man grunted again, and this time Fargo could smell the whiskey on his breath. He had enemies among the members of the expedition, no doubt about that. He didn't know which one this man was, but he was confident that it must be either Prescott, Baird, or one of the others attacking him. The only one he ruled out was Strayhorn, who was injured too badly to brawl like this.

The man must have seen him walking Victoria to the coach and then followed him back out here to jump him. Liquor had given the hombre the courage to launch his attack. But the man wasn't so drunk that he couldn't fight. He feinted with the club and then aimed a kick at Fargo's groin. Fargo twisted aside just in time to take the blow on his thigh. It was still powerful enough to knock him back a couple of steps and make his leg go numb. He lost his balance and fell.

The man charged again, sweeping the club up and then down. Fargo rolled aside and heard a sharp crack as the club slammed into the ground and broke. That could have been his skull cracking if he had been just a little slower, he thought.

With his good leg, he snapped a kick that caught the other man on the knee. The man staggered back, cursing under his breath.

Fargo rolled over and leaped up as feeling began to return to his numbed leg. He had the Colt on his hip and could have ended this fracas with a shot, but he was willing to meet his opponent on equal terms. The man hadn't brought gunplay into this, and neither would Fargo unless he had to.

With a snarl, the man tossed the broken branch aside. He reached to his waist, and Fargo saw moonlight glitter on cold steel as the man advanced on him with a knife in his hand. The blade weaved back and forth a little in the manner of an experienced knife fighter.

This man, whoever he was, wasn't the only one who had crossed steel with enemies in the past. Fargo bent and plucked the Arkansas toothpick from the sheath strapped to his calf.

He straightened in time to parry the first slash that the man aimed at his face. Steel rang sharply against steel. Fargo made a thrust of his own, but the man turned it aside with his blade. Then he swung a backhand slash at the Trailsman. Fargo avoided the knife with a quick step back.

So far they were just feeling each other out, trying to gauge each other's strengths and weaknesses. Fargo's opponent was fast and handled a blade well. Fargo had faced better knife fighters, however. He felt like he could win this fight as long as luck didn't turn against him. The swiftly shifting tides of fortune were always difficult to predict.

The man lunged forward, the knife whipping back and forth in his hand. Fargo was forced to parry once, twice, three times. The last slash was just a feint, though, and the blade suddenly dropped and darted forward. Fargo twisted. The tip of the knife tore through the tough buckskin shirt and traced a fiery line on his side. Fargo grunted in pain and shifted, turning even more. He made a thrust of his own. When the man blocked it, Fargo threw his left fist in a punch that thudded home against the man's jaw.

Caught by surprise, the man went down. But then he rolled over and came right back up, slashing with his knife so that Fargo couldn't close in on him. Fargo was forced to draw back and take a moment to catch his breath. The cut in his side hurt and he felt blood trickling from it, but the wound wasn't bad enough to slow him down. It was more of an annoyance than anything else.

The blades struck sparks from each other as they came together and leaped apart. The noise of the clash had reached the camp by now, and several men came running toward the trees to see what was going on. Fargo heard their shouts and the thud of their footsteps, but he couldn't afford to take his attention off his opponent—not when the man was so fast and deadly. Again, Fargo had to react quickly to parry an attack.

The man was moving a little slower now, though. He had been on the offensive for most of this fight, and it was wearing him out. Losing speed and strength in the middle of a knife fight was dangerous, and the man had to know it. Fargo sensed a little desperation in the man's movements as he thrust and hacked with the big knife in his hand.

Fargo parried, circled, then thrust his own knife. The Arkansas toothpick got through and bit into the man's arm. He cried out in pain.

"Drop the knife," Fargo urged. "Give it up."

"Go to hell!" the man shot back at him. He attacked again, injured arm and all.

Fargo darted aside. "Let it go," he said. "I don't want to kill you."

"I ain't the one who's gonna die!"

Suddenly, the man shifted his grip on the knife and threw himself forward, bringing his arm up and around in an overhand blow. The blade would have ripped Fargo in half if it had landed, but he leaped aside to avoid the killing stroke.

At the same time, he dropped the toothpick and

kept twisting, reaching up to grab the man's knife wrist as the blade passed harmlessly over Fargo's shoulder. Fargo threw his hip into the man's body and heaved on his arm. With a startled cry, the man went up and over, flying through the air as a result of the wrestling throw.

He landed heavily on the ground, rolled over, and spasmed as he let out a thin scream. Fargo bent and snatched the Arkansas toothpick from the ground in case he still needed to defend himself. But it quickly became obvious that the man wasn't going to be getting up to continue the fight. He writhed for a moment and then lay still.

Fargo became aware that the men from the camp were gathered around him and his fallen opponent. Somebody struck a match. The foul scent of the lucifer filled the air. The flickering yellow glow lighted the area under the trees and revealed the sprawled body of the man called Baird. The handle of a Bowie knife jutted up from his belly where he had fallen on it and driven the blade deep into his vitals. Baird's eyes were wide open, staring in shock and horror—and frozen that way forever because life had departed from them.

Several men crowded forward, among them Prescott. "You bastard!" he growled at Fargo. "You killed him!" He started to reach for his gun.

Jeb Tolbert lunged at him and grabbed his arm, stopping the draw from being accomplished. "Hold it, you damned fool!" he snapped. "We all saw what happened. Fargo tried to get Baird to give it up. Baird just wouldn't do it!"

Fargo's hand was on the butt of his Colt. He would have drawn if Prescott had forced the issue, but he was grateful to Tolbert for stepping in and stopping the shoot-out before it could start.

"Yeah," Bart Stanton put in. "Baird fell on his knife when Fargo threw him. It was an accident, that's all."

"Nothing accidental about it," Prescott argued hotly. "Fargo wanted to kill him."

"I didn't want him to kill *me*," Fargo said. "There's a difference. Baird had a chance to drop his knife."

Prescott just glared at him. Clearly, nothing anybody could say to him was going to change his mind about what had happened.

The area under the trees got brighter as several more men walked up, one of them carrying a lantern. Fargo saw that it was Angus McAllister. Richard Francis Olney was beside him.

"Here, now," said McAllister. "What's all this, eh?"

"My God!" Olney exclaimed. "That's Baird lying on the ground. He . . . he appears to be dead."

"That's because Fargo killed him," Prescott grated out. He jerked his arm free from Tolbert's grip. "And these old fossils you hired seem to think that's all right."

"What happened here?" Olney asked crisply, more in possession of himself now. The sight of Baird's bloody corpse had thrown him for a moment.

"I told you they might try to settle the score," Fargo said.

"You mean this man attacked you, Mr. Fargo?"

"That's exactly what I mean." Fargo lifted a hand to his head and gingerly touched a lump that was forming above his left ear. "He tried to bash my brains out with a broken tree limb. Then when that didn't work, he took a knife after me."

Olney swung toward Prescott. "You were Baird's friend, Prescott. Did you know he was planning to attack Mr. Fargo?"

"I didn't know a damned thing about it," Prescott answered sullenly. "But I wish he'd busted the bastard's skull open."

Prescott's claim of ignorance didn't convince Fargo. He thought there was a good chance Prescott had prodded Baird into the attack.

"That's quite enough of that kind of talk." Olney turned back to Fargo. "My apologies, Mr. Fargo. Clearly, you were attacked, and you had every right to defend yourself. It's regrettable that Baird lost his life, but no one blames you for that." Olney glanced meaningfully at Prescott, who just glowered back stubbornly.

Fargo looked around and spotted his hat lying on the ground where it had been knocked off his head in Baird's initial attack. He picked it up, knocked dirt and pine needles off it, and settled it back on his head. "I'm sorry about Baird," he said. "I don't take pleasure in a man dying, no matter who he is."

"Of course," Olney answered. "Some of you men tend to the body. Prepare it for burial the first thing in the morning. And let me be clear about this: No one is to bother Mr. Fargo. This is over. Is that plain enough?"

There were mutters of agreement from a few of the men. Prescott and Barnett didn't say anything, however.

The knot of men under the trees broke up. Most of Olney's men went back to camp. Fargo, Olney, McAllister, and the two mountain men walked over to the trading post.

"Again, I can't tell you how sorry I am about this, Mr. Fargo," Olney said. "I know that many of the men I've employed on this expedition are, well, rather rough in nature. It seemed to me that such men were just what I needed to deal with any dangers we might encounter. Perhaps I should have thought that through a bit more."

"Too late now," Fargo said. "But I reckon it's just the real hotheads, like Prescott, that you have to worry about."

"Bart and me will keep an eye on 'em as best we can, Mr. Olney," Tolbert promised. "Can't watch 'em twenty-four hours a day, though. If they're bound and determined to get up to some mischief, we may not be able to stop 'em."

"Perhaps what I should do," Olney said, "is to discharge Prescott, Barnett, Strayhorn, and Mitchell." He looked at Fargo. "Those are the only ones who have clashed directly with you, isn't that right?"

Fargo nodded. "That would leave you short-handed, though."

"I'm sure that if you agreed to work for me, it would more than make up for any loss."

A grin spread slowly across Fargo's face. That was neatly done on Olney's part, he thought. "I don't think so," he said.

"I hope you'll reconsider. For now, I'll bid you all good night and say, once again, that I'm sorry for the incident."

"Forget it," Fargo said. "I'm still breathing. That's more than Baird can say."

Olney nodded and left the trading post. Once he was gone, Elizabeth came over to Fargo and said worriedly, "You've been bleeding, Skye. I can see it on your shirt."

"It's just a scratch," Fargo assured her.

"Well, take that shirt off anyway so I can tend to it."

Her tone didn't leave any room for argument.

McAllister chuckled and said, "Ye might as well do wha' she says, laddie. Once that gal o' mine makes her mind up, there's no changin' it."

Tolbert said, "We'll be gettin' back to camp." He and Stanton followed Olney out the door, leaving Fargo alone with the McAllisters.

He peeled his shirt up and over his head, revealing the long, narrow cut in his side. It had bled some, but not too badly.

"I'll clean that up and put some ointment on it," Elizabeth said. "Sit down at the table, Skye."

McAllister and Andrew went back to the living quarters in the rear of the trading post, leaving Fargo and Elizabeth alone. She cleaned the wound with a cloth and some warm water and then leaned close to him to apply some medicinal ointment to the cut. As she did, she lifted her head suddenly.

"What's that scent?" she asked. "It smells like . . . Mrs. Arrowsmith's perfume?"

Then her eyes widened with realization and she stared at Fargo, her face gradually darkening with anger.

Fargo wasn't in the habit of defending himself from jealous women. He hadn't made any promises to Elizabeth McAllister. But he did sort of wish at this moment that Victoria's perfume hadn't lingered on him so that Elizabeth's keen nose could detect it.

"You were attacked while you were coming back from walking Mrs. Arrowsmith to her coach, weren't you?"

Fargo nodded. "That's right."

"It must have taken you quite a while to get her there."

"It took a while keeping Baird from killing me."

Elizabeth just sniffed angrily. She straightened from what she had been doing and said, "I don't think you need a bandage for that cut."

"Fine," Fargo said. He stood and picked up his shirt. The wound in his side twinged a little as he pulled the garment back over his head, but he didn't show any sign of it on his face.

"Good night," Elizabeth said coolly. She turned and walked toward the rear of the trading post.

Fargo let her go. He didn't owe her any explanations or apologies. He would have preferred that she wasn't angry with him, but that was her own choice.

One thing about it, he mused as he went out to the shed—the question of whom Elizabeth had been jealous of earlier had now been answered.

The rest of the night passed peacefully, and Fargo was grateful for that. His side was a little stiff when he got up the next morning, but it wasn't too bad. A day or two and he would be back to normal, he knew.

Elizabeth was still cool toward him at breakfast. After eating, Fargo walked over to the camp. Tolbert and Stanton sat beside the fire, sipping from cups of coffee.

"Mornin', Fargo," Tolbert greeted him. "Want some coffee and vittles?"

"I've eaten already," Fargo said. "I was looking more for company than anything else."

"Well, sit a spell," Stanton invited. He waved a hand toward the log where he and Tolbert were seated.

Fargo joined them. "Any more trouble last night?" he asked quietly.

Tolbert shook his head. "Not really. Prescott ran his mouth some, but nobody paid much attention to him, not even Barnett and Mitchell. I get the feelin' they're ready to let go of their grudge against you, Fargo. Prescott's the only one who's still burnin' up inside over what happened."

Fargo nodded, not surprised by what he had just heard. Men like the hardcases Olney had hired had a certain amount of loyalty to each other, but it didn't go very far. They had signed on for the money, and when you got right down to it, that was all they really cared about. That, and taking care of their own hides.

He heard what sounded like the cough of a mountain lion from one of the wagons. "What have you got in there?" he asked as he nodded toward the vehicles with their specially constructed cages.

Stanton grinned. "Come take a look."

The three men got to their feet and strolled over to the wagons. Being careful not to get too close, Fargo peered through the openings between the slats, which he now saw were reinforced with iron straps.

"I thought I heard a mountain lion," he said as he watched a big, tawny cat pace back and forth as much as it could in the close confines of the cage. "How in the world did you ever manage to catch one alive?"

"It weren't easy—I can tell you that," Tolbert replied with a grin. "We rigged a snare that hung him up by his back feet when he stepped in it. Then we had to rope his front legs and his head. Those cages got doors on top of them, so we heisted the catamount up high enough in the air so's the wagon could be driven under him. Then we lowered him down in there, closed it up, and drove off. Had to work the ropes off him later with poles and hooks. It's a tricky business all the way around, no matter how you look at it."

"Even bein' careful, a couple of fellas nearly got clawed bad," Stanton put in.

The back of each wagon was divided into three separate pens. Fargo moved on to the next one, looked inside, and said, "Good Lord! That's a grizzly cub!"

"Yeah, and we were damn lucky to grab the little

varmint and get out of there before the mama bear came back. That little fella will grow up in Philadelphia, not in the Rocky Mountains.''

Fargo felt a twinge of sadness when Tolbert said that. It didn't seem right somehow. Of course, if not for what Olney was doing, folks back in Philadelphia would never get the chance to see a live grizzly bear. But if they wanted to see such a thing badly enough, they could come out here and take a gander for themselves, couldn't they?

Most of them couldn't, Fargo realized. They would never have that chance. But was it worth depriving that bear cub of the life he had been destined to lead just so a bunch of people could come and gawk at him?

Fargo didn't know the answer. He just knew he had more in common with the bear cub than he did with the people who would come to Olney's zoological garden to look at it.

The other cages held an assortment of smaller animals—beaver, muskrats, porcupines—and even a few birds.

"What else are you after?" Fargo asked when he had looked at all of the animals.

"Mr. Olney says he'd like to get a timber wolf if he can," Tolbert said.

"And maybe a moose," Stanton added. "And anything else we can find that'll impress the folks back in Philadelphia.''

"Well, I'm glad the job belongs to you boys and not to me," Fargo said.

"We were sort of hoping you'd take Mr. Olney up on his job offer. It'd be a heap easier if we had the Trailsman along with us."

Fargo shook his head. "I can't do anything you fellas can't do. You know the trails, and you've probably done a lot more trapping than I have. I never would've thought of roping a mountain lion and lowering him into a cage."

"Actually, that was Mr. Olney's idea," Tolbert said. "He's mighty smart about things like that."

Fargo was surprised. Olney had struck him as a pompous little blowhard. Obviously, the man had some intelligence and initiative, since he had come up with a method of capturing a mountain lion alive.

"I think I'll pass on the offer, anyway," Fargo said. "I can't say I'm too fond of the idea of taking all these critters back east and keeping them in cages."

Tolbert frowned. "I know what you mean. It don't hardly seem right. But the pay's good, and it ain't really hurtin' the animals."

"Funny, though," Stanton mused. "Sometimes I feel like puttin' 'em in cages is worse than killin' them for their pelts."

Fargo knew just how the mountain man felt. He nodded in agreement.

With his curiosity satisfied, he walked back over to the camp fire with Tolbert and Stanton. "How long do you reckon you'll be here?" he asked.

Tolbert shook his head. "Don't rightly know. Until Mr. Olney's satisfied, I guess. A few days, maybe a week?"

"What are you going to do, Fargo?" asked Stanton.

"I'll stay on with the McAllisters," Fargo said. "I still don't trust Prescott."

Tolbert said, "We'll keep an eye on him, if you want to be movin' on."

"I know, but I'll feel better if I'm here."

"That McAllister gal is mighty pretty," Stanton said with a grin. "Kind of odd, though, the way she looks like an Injun and sounds white."

"Elizabeth's not the reason I'm staying on. Not the

110

only reason, anyway. The boy, Andrew, has it in his head that he wants to run off to the plains and hunt buffalo. That's what he thinks an Indian ought to do."

Tolbert took out his pipe. "Bein' a youngster that age is confusin' enough to start with, without havin' to worry about whether you're Injun or white. No wonder the boy sulls up like a possum."

Andrew wasn't the only one who was sullen this morning, Fargo thought as he said good-bye to the two buckskinners and walked back to the trading post. Elizabeth was still angry with him over what she thought had happened between him and Victoria Arrowsmith. Of course, she was pretty much right in her suspicions, even though she didn't know the details, but that didn't make Fargo feel any better.

Elizabeth would get over it, he told himself. Besides, he didn't intend to spend any more time alone with Victoria, so that ought to help the situation. He didn't feel that he owed Elizabeth any explanations or apologies, but he wasn't going to go out of his way to antagonize her, either.

When he arrived at the trading post, he saw that he wasn't going to have to. Victoria was already taking care of that herself.

Fargo hadn't seen Victoria going over to the trading post, but she was there, trying to engage Elizabeth in small talk. Elizabeth coldly ignored her. Things were just the opposite of the way they had been the day before. Elizabeth had followed Victoria around like a puppy, wanting to know everything possible about life back east in Philadelphia. Now it was Victoria trying to engage her in conversation, only to be rebuffed.

"Really, I don't know why you're upset with me, Elizabeth," Victoria was saying as Fargo entered the trading post. "I haven't done anything to you."

Elizabeth just sniffed and turned away, pointedly

111

putting her back to Victoria as she worked moving a stack of bolts of colorful cloth from one counter to another to make some room.

Victoria put her hands on her hips and said in exasperation, "Well!" She became aware of Fargo standing behind her and turned toward him, her look of frustration vanishing in a smile of greeting. Her voice was lilting as she said, "Good morning, Skye!"

Fargo saw Elizabeth's back stiffen. Victoria wasn't helping matters any.

It was about to get worse. Victoria stepped over to Fargo, put her arms around him, and planted a big kiss on his mouth.

Fargo probably could have stopped her. Probably *should* have stopped her, he thought. But she had taken him by surprise, acting so brazenly right here in the trading post in front of Elizabeth.

Elizabeth turned, saw Victoria plastered to Fargo, and turned pale. She dropped the bolt of cloth she was holding.

The kiss was long and passionate. Fargo didn't push her away, and he wouldn't have been human if he hadn't reacted to what she was doing to him. She must have felt his reaction, because there was a satisfied smirk on her face when she finally broke the kiss and moved back a little.

"That was wonderful," she said breathlessly. "Even better than last night."

Then Victoria turned and smiled at Elizabeth, and that was the last straw.

With a howl of anger, Elizabeth launched herself at Victoria, her hands reaching for the older woman's throat.

8

Fargo stood his ground as Elizabeth crashed into Victoria and knocked her backward. Both women would have sprawled to the puncheon floor if Fargo hadn't been there to grab them. "Hold it!" he said as he tried to get between them. "Damn it, Elizabeth—"

At that moment, Elizabeth gave up on the idea of getting her hands around Victoria's neck and strangling her. She threw a punch instead, balling her right hand into a small, hard fist.

When she had first come running into Fargo's camp several days earlier and he had grabbed her to stop her mad flight, she had tried to punch him. He had been able to avoid those blows. This one he didn't see coming because it was aimed at Victoria. But when Victoria jerked her head aside, Elizabeth's fist shot over her shoulder and smacked into Fargo's throat instead.

The punch took him more by surprise than hurt him. But for a moment, as he took a step backward, he couldn't get his breath.

That gave Victoria time to grab Elizabeth's long black hair and jerk on it. Elizabeth screamed in pain and anger and retaliated by grabbing Victoria's coppery hair and pulling hard on it. Victoria screeched, too.

Locked together, they reeled across the floor and crashed into a set of shelves that tipped over and toppled with a smash. Elizabeth left off pulling Victoria's hair and tried to claw her eyes out instead. Victoria fended her off with one hand and flailed wild punches with the other.

Their feet then tangled up with each other and they went down, landing hard on the floor. That wasn't enough to knock them apart, however. They rolled across the floor, still wrestling and screaming.

Angus McAllister came running from the back of the trading post, trailed by Andrew. "Great God A'mighty!" the Scotsman shouted. "Wha' th' devil is all that caterwaulin'?"

He stopped so short when he saw the women fighting on the floor that Andrew ran into him from behind and almost knocked him down. Fargo stood on the other side of the battle, rubbing his throat where Elizabeth had punched him.

McAllister looked at Fargo and asked over the din. "Should we do ought to stop this fracas?"

"I'm not sure I want to get in the middle of it, Angus," Fargo said honestly. He had faced down plenty of dangers in his life, but trying to break up a brawl between two women, while not unique in his experience, was sure as hell rare.

But Elizabeth and Victoria might do some serious damage to each other if they weren't stopped. Fargo stepped closer and told McAllister, "Grab Elizabeth! I'll get Mrs. Arrowsmith!"

He waited a second for a good opportunity, then bent forward and got his arms around Victoria. With a grunt of effort, he lifted her, pulling her away from Elizabeth.

Fargo then turned, swinging Victoria's feet off the floor and holding her that way. She kicked her legs and swung her arms, and spit furious, incoherent words. It was a little like trying to hang on to a bobcat, thought Fargo.

McAllister got hold of Elizabeth and tugged her toward the rear of the trading post. "Gi' me a hand here, Andrew!" he snapped. "Yer sister's got her dander up, she does!"

Fargo carried Victoria all the way to the front door before he put her down. McAllister and Andrew wrestled Elizabeth over to the counter that ran across the back of the room. The two women faced each other along the length of the aisle between the shelves, each one trying to out-glare the other one.

"Settle down!" Fargo said sharply. "And I mean both of you, damn it!"

"She started it!" Elizabeth cried, pointing a trembling finger at Victoria.

"I did no such thing!" Victoria protested. "I merely told Skye good morning."

"You redheaded Eastern trollop!"

"Filthy redskinned savage!"

Fargo took a deep breath and bellowed, "Shut the hell up!" He was embarrassed for the two of them and angry at their lack of self-control. It made things even worse that they were basically fighting over him. Neither one of them had a right to do that.

Victoria looked shocked at the vehemence of his reaction. "Skye, I was just . . . just . . ."

"You ought to be ashamed of yourself." He looked across the room at Elizabeth. "And so should you. Neither of you acted much like a lady."

"I'm *not* a lady!" Elizabeth flared. "I am a woman of the Bannock tribe!"

"*Now* you want to be an Indian, instead of a prissy white lady," Andrew muttered.

Fargo frowned at him. Comments like that were liable to just make matters worse.

Elizabeth ignored her brother, though. She was too mad at Victoria to allow anything to distract her. "I don't understand what you see in her anyway, Skye," she said. "She's old and ugly!"

Victoria was neither of those things, but Fargo didn't figure this was a good time to point that out.

Before he could say anything, however, Victoria sniffed and said, "I imagine Skye found my affections to be a welcome change from rutting with squaws who stink of bear grease, as I assume he's been doing with you!"

"Here now!" McAllister roared. "I'll thank ye to keep a civil tongue in yer head, missus. That be my daughter ye're talkin' about!" Then he frowned, shook his head, and went on. "Wait just a minute. Who said anythin' about ruttin'? Fargo, wha' th' devil is she talkin' about?"

Fargo's teeth ground together. This situation was going from bad to worse in a hurry.

The door of the trading post opened, and Richard Francis Olney hurried in, an excited look on his face. "What's all the commotion?" he wanted to know. "We heard the shouting all the way over at camp—"

He stopped short as he saw his sister standing there, her hair disheveled and her face set in rigid lines of outrage. Fargo's left arm was still around her waist, holding her in case she tried to charge Elizabeth.

"Mr. Fargo!" Olney exclaimed. "I'll thank you to unhand my sister!"

"Gladly," Fargo growled. He turned and thrust Victoria into Olney's arms. "*You* hang on to her!"

Flustered to find his arms full of his own sister, Olney clumsily disentangled himself and stepped between Fargo and Victoria. She glowered over his shoulder, but she didn't try to get around him and renew her attack.

"I'm still waitin' for an answer, Fargo," Angus McAllister said.

Elizabeth turned to him and said, "Leave him alone, Pa. It's not like Skye is the first man who ever did anything like that with me."

McAllister's eyes widened. "Wha' . . . wha' are ye sayin', lass? Dinna I raise ye to be a good Christian lass?"

"You didn't raise me to be a nun!"

"Well, maybe I should have! Good Lord, I never thought—"

"Never thought that I'm a grown woman now— that's what you never thought!"

Fargo looked through the open door and saw Jeb Tolbert and Bart Stanton standing on the porch with big grins on their faces. They must have followed Olney over here to see what the uproar was all about, and they seemed to be enjoying themselves immensely. Fargo was torn between wanting to wipe those grins off their faces and joining in their amusement at his own expense. He had gotten himself in some awkward fixes before, but this was one of the most ludicrous.

"All right," he said sharply, cutting through the hubbub in the trading post. "Olney, take your sister back to your camp and keep her there."

"I don't think you're in any position to be giving orders, Mr. Fargo," Olney said coldly. When Fargo's eyes narrowed, though, he took a step back and went on. "But everyone does need to calm down, and that can be accomplished more easily if Victoria and I leave." He turned and took her arm. "Come along, Victoria."

She was just about as big as he was, and Fargo wouldn't have been surprised if she'd hauled off and walloped him one. Instead, she let him steer her out of the trading post, although she threw a fierce glare over her shoulder as she was leaving. Fargo couldn't tell if the look was directed at him or Elizabeth, or both of them. Probably the latter, he thought.

Fargo turned to McAllister. "Angus, you need to have a talk with your daughter."

"Aye, it seems that I do." The trader glared at Fargo. "An' it's no' too sure I am that ye're welcome here anymore, mister."

"We can talk about that later," Fargo said. "Right now, everybody just needs to take a deep breath and calm down."

"Mr. Olney was right about one thing. . . . Ye're mighty free wi' them orders ye're givin'."

"Somebody's got to keep a cool head about this."

Elizabeth sniffed loudly and contemptuously. She turned and marched around the counter, disappearing through a door into the living quarters in the rear. McAllister followed her, shaking his head.

That left Andrew to stand there and say, "Are you sure you don't want to go hunt buffalo with me, Mr. Fargo?"

Fargo had to admit that, right now, it didn't sound like such a bad idea.

Fargo sat on the front porch of the trading post for a while with Tolbert and Stanton, listening to the two mountain men making jokes at his expense. He couldn't blame them for finding the situation funny. Fate had seemingly blessed him with the ability to stumble onto beautiful women wherever he went, but this time it had sort of backfired on him.

Eventually, Tolbert and Stanton stood up, and Tolbert said, "I reckon we'd better get back over there and see if Mr. Olney wants us to go out scoutin' for animals today."

" 'Specimens,' he calls 'em," Stanton put in. "Poor varmints is more like it."

"You could quit if you don't like what he's doing," Fargo pointed out. He wasn't in a very sympathetic mood at the moment.

"Sure we could, but he's payin' us more than we earned some whole years at trappin'," Tolbert said. "It's hard to turn down good wages."

Fargo nodded, even though on many occasions in the past, he had refused lucrative job offers because he didn't like what he would have had to do to earn the money.

The buckskinners walked off toward the wagons. Fargo went out to the shed and spent some time brushing and combing the Ovaro. That's what he was doing when Angus McAllister found him.

"I've come to have that talk wi' ye," the trader began. "I still appreciate wha' ye done for me children, but I don't want ye around here no more, Fargo."

Fargo faced the Scotsman. "Because of Elizabeth, you mean?"

"Aye. That be exactly wha' I mean."

"You realize that she's a grown woman, don't you?"

McAllister looked pained. "Aye. There be times when I sorta forget that, but I ken that Elizabeth is grown. An' I ken, too, that ye ain't th' only one to blame for wha' happened. But still, I'd sleep more sound of a night if ye weren't around here no more."

"So be it," Fargo said with a nod. "I'll ride out today."

McAllister returned his nod curtly and turned to stalk back to the trading post.

Fargo began getting the stallion ready to ride. He would comply with McAllister's wishes and leave the trading post . . . but he wasn't going to go very far. He didn't trust Prescott and the other hardcases who had been hired by Olney. Tolbert and Stanton had promised to do their best to keep the men in line, but there were only two of them.

There were plenty of places close by in the hills where Fargo could keep an eye on the situation until Olney's party had moved on. If there was no trouble, McAllister wouldn't know that he was anywhere around.

A short time later, after Fargo had the Ovaro saddled, McAllister came back out to the shed carrying a canvas sack. "I brung ye some supplies," he said as he held out the sack. "Like I told ye, I appreciate wha' ye done for me family."

Fargo took the provisions and hung the sack on his saddle. "I'm obliged to you," he said.

"No, ye ain't. Ye saved th' lives o' me children, an' that be a debt I can ne'er repay. So we ain't square an' we never will be, but this is th' best I can do."

Fargo nodded in understanding. He swung up into the saddle.

"Will you say good-bye to them for me?" he asked.

McAllister hesitated and then said grudgingly, "Aye."

"Thanks." Fargo started to turn the Ovaro, but he paused and added, "Keep a close eye on that bunch down by the river. You can trust Tolbert and Stanton. I'm not sure about any of the rest of them."

"I didna live as long as I have by trustin' too much," McAllister assured him.

Fargo nodded again and heeled the stallion into a trot. He rode west, into the foothills of the Madison Range. The mountains loomed above him, gray and purple and snowcapped, dominating the landscape. He was out of sight of the trading post in a matter of minutes.

As soon as he could no longer be seen from the river, Fargo rode around a hill and then up the far slope. When he reached the crest, he dismounted and led the stallion through the trees until he could look down and see the trading post below him and about half a mile away. This would make a good spot for his camp, he thought. From here he could watch both the trading post and Olney's camp, and he was close enough to hear gunshots if any more trouble broke out. He left the Ovaro saddled for the time being and settled down to wait.

Later in the morning, Tolbert, Stanton, and some of the other men rode out, no doubt on a scouting mission to locate more animals for Olney to take back to Philadelphia with him. With the two mountain men gone, Fargo watched the camp even more closely, but none of the hardcases approached the trading post. Maybe they were following Olney's orders not to make any more trouble.

The day passed quietly enough. Fargo dozed a couple of times and enjoyed the peace and beauty of the high country. He ate a cold lunch of jerky from his saddlebags and a couple of biscuits from the sack of supplies Angus McAllister had given him. Tolbert, Stanton, and the other men rode back late in the afternoon. As nightfall approached, Fargo unsaddled the Ovaro and spread his bedroll on the ground. He had the ability to sleep well, no matter where he was.

Darkness had fallen and Fargo was already curled in his blankets when he heard a faint noise nearby and the Ovaro suddenly let out a whinny. Instantly, Fargo threw the blankets aside and rolled over. He came up in a crouch with the Colt in his hand.

A gasp and a hurried exclamation of "Skye!" in a familiar voice made him hold off on the trigger. He stood and holstered the gun.

"What are you doing here, Elizabeth?" he asked flatly.

"I followed you, of course." She stepped closer, close enough so that he could make her out in the stray beams of starlight that slanted through the trees over their heads. "I knew you wouldn't go very far."

"That doesn't explain why you're here."

She came even closer. "Damn it, Skye . . . why did you leave?"

"Your father asked me to, and I thought honoring his wishes was the right thing to do."

"Even though I didn't want you to go?"

Fargo couldn't help but chuckle. "This morning it didn't seem much like you wanted me around."

"Don't laugh at me!" she said with a flash of anger. "I still haven't forgiven you for whatever you did with that redheaded bitch. . . . Or maybe I have. . . . I don't know."

Fargo heard the confusion in her voice. She couldn't make up her mind how she felt. He seldom experienced such doubts himself, but he could still sympathize with Elizabeth.

"I reckon you snuck out of the trading post," he said.

"That's right. Pa would be furious with me if he knew I was up here."

"Then you should go on back home now," Fargo told her. "Your father is a good man, and he worries about you."

"He worries too much."

"I don't know anything about raising youngsters," Fargo said, "but I'm not sure it's possible to worry too much when you have kids."

"I'm *not* a kid!"

As if to emphasize that point, she moved even closer and put her arms around his neck. Her firm breasts pressed against his chest, and her pelvis thrust against his groin. Even in the darkness, her mouth unerringly found his. Her lips were hot and wet and parted eagerly as she boldly slipped her tongue into his mouth.

Fargo's shaft hardened in response to the sensual delights washing over him. Elizabeth felt his erection prodding her belly and that prompted her to grind even harder against him. When she finally broke the long, passionate kiss, Fargo had to agree: "No, you're no kid—that's for sure."

"I . . . I think I'm still mad at you, Skye," Elizabeth whispered, "but make love to me anyway!"

Fargo sank down onto his blankets, pulling her with him. This might be a mistake, he reflected fleetingly, but Elizabeth was not going to be denied.

He stretched out with her lying on top of him, and they kissed and caressed each other for long moments before their arousal grew so strong that they had to start getting their clothing out of the way. It was easy for Fargo to slip off Elizabeth's buckskin dress. She unfastened his trousers and pulled them and his underwear off when he lifted his hips from the ground. Then he sat up and she peeled the buckskin shirt up and over his head. When they were both nude, the cool night air should have been chilly on their bare skin, but excitement had heated them up to the point that they didn't notice the temperature.

They embraced and kissed again. Fargo's hands explored every sweeping curve, every intimate nook and cranny of Elizabeth's body. At the same time, her hands were busy stroking his long, thick member and cupping the heavy sac at its base.

After a while, Elizabeth swung around so that she was facing away from Fargo and straddled his chest with her legs. Then she bent forward to grip his shaft with both hands and take the head into her mouth. She was in perfect position for Fargo to reach up, spread the folds of her sex with his thumbs, and spear his tongue into her heated core. Elizabeth's hips jerked in response.

Fargo licked and sucked her until climax after climax shuddered through her. Despite the spasms that rocked her, she managed to keep his shaft in her mouth. The exquisite sensations that her oral caresses brought to him had him shaking, too. It took all of his willpower to keep from emptying himself down her throat.

Finally, Elizabeth collapsed in sated exhaustion with her head resting on his groin and his still-throbbing shaft brushing her cheek. She lay there catching her breath while Fargo kissed the inside of her thighs and stroked his fingers through the long, silky black hair that covered her mound.

After a few minutes, what he was doing began to excite her again. She pushed herself up, pausing on the way to bestow a kiss on the head of his shaft, and then turned around again so that her hips were poised above his. She grasped his manhood and brought the tip of it to her opening, where she rubbed it back and forth for a moment in the hot slickness that had drenched her.

Then she lowered herself slowly onto him, taking him inside her inch by maddening inch.

After what seemed like a pleasure-filled eternity, Fargo's member was fully embedded within her, completely sheathed so that the tip touched the back wall of her female cavity. "Oh!" she gasped. "No one has ever . . . ever filled me like this! Oh, Skye!"

She bent down and kissed him again. Fargo held her tenderly. Neither of them moved yet. They were content to be so completely joined.

But then Elizabeth's hips began to rock back and forth a little, and Fargo's hips lifted from the ground as he thrust into her. They quickly fell into a timeless rhythm. Elizabeth sat up straight so that she could pump harder. Fargo reached up to fill his palms with the firm, bronzed globes of her breasts. His thumbs found the dark brown nipples and stroked them.

The pace of their lovemaking steadily increased. Fargo's arousal had built to the point that he knew his climax was imminent. There would be no holding it back this time. He shifted his hands from Elizabeth's breasts to her hips so that he could steady her as he drove harder and faster into her. She braced herself by resting her hands on his chest. Her fingers dug into his flesh as she panted in excitement.

Then Fargo surged up into her one final time and let go, flooding her with his seed. Elizabeth shuddered heavily as a fresh climax rippled through her at the same moment.

When it was over, she fell forward onto his chest. Fargo cradled her there, stroking her long hair that spread out around their heads like a sable cloud.

Fargo had no doubt in his mind that something this good was the right thing to do.

Elizabeth seemed satisfied, too. She sighed deeply. "I'm glad you didn't leave completely, Skye," she whispered. "I hope you'll stay for a while."

"I'll be around until Olney's bunch moves on," Fargo said. "They didn't cause any more problems today, did they?"

Elizabeth lifted her head. "No, none of them even came back over to the trading post except for Mr. Tolbert and Mr. Stanton, and my father likes them."

She didn't say anything about Victoria, so Fargo figured it would be wise not to even bring up that subject. Leave well enough alone, he thought.

"Mr. Tolbert said they found some wolf sign, so they'll try to catch one of them before they move on," Elizabeth continued. "It bothers me a little, the way they have those animals caged up."

"I'm not too fond of it myself," admitted Fargo.

"Still, I can't imagine living in a place where there aren't any animals. I might like to visit Philadelphia, but I couldn't ever live there."

Fargo understood that and would have said as much if something else hadn't happened at that moment. Down below in the valley, the sudden rattle of gunfire shattered the peaceful night.

Elizabeth jerked her head up and exclaimed, "My God! Skye, what—"

Fargo was already rolling out from under her and reaching for his trousers and the holstered Colt. He pulled the trousers on, jerked the revolver from its holster, and ran over to the edge of the trees so that he could look down at the trading post. As he stopped, Elizabeth padded up beside him, still nude.

Fargo saw muzzle flashes blooming like orange flowers in the darkness around the trading post. With a great roar, a thick tongue of flame lashed out from the porch, and Fargo knew that was Angus McAllister opening fire with his shotgun. The place was under attack. It seemed to Fargo that the only ones who could be carrying out the assault were the men from Olney's camp.

"Stay here," Fargo told Elizabeth. He swung around, intending to grab the Ovaro and ride down there bareback. He didn't know exactly what was going on, but he intended to be in the thick of it—whatever it was, doing whatever he could to set things right.

Before he could reach the stallion, though, Fargo heard the big black-and-white horse give a shrill whinny of anger. The Ovaro reared up and lashed out with his front hooves at shadowy shapes moving under the trees. A man's voice yelled, "Watch out!"

Whoever those men were, Fargo knew they were up to no good. He leveled the Colt and shouted, "Hold it!"

"It's Fargo! Kill him!"

That removed any lingering doubts. Fargo reared back the hammer and fired. Smoke and flame geysered from the barrel of the Colt.

The attackers, apparently two or three of them, threw lead back. He dropped to one knee and triggered twice more, hoping that Elizabeth had enough sense to get down and crawl away as fast as she could. He didn't want to call out to her, because the gunmen might not know she was up here. She would have a better chance to get away if he didn't call attention to her.

Fargo dove to the side as a slug sizzled past his ear. He rolled over and came up in a crouch as he saw another pair of muzzle flashes and more lead fanged at him. He aimed at one of the flashes and squeezed the trigger, and a hoarse yell of pain rewarded him.

His satisfaction was fleeting, however. In the next instant, what felt like the side of a mountain reared up and slammed him on the side of the head. He went over backward, skyrockets exploding in his brain. That brilliant display lasted only a second before it was swept away by utter blackness.

Fargo was swept away, too, and the last thing he was aware of was the sound of Elizabeth McAllister screaming.

9

The pain was good, because it meant he was still alive. Although, Fargo told himself, it could just mean that he was in Hell, because he figured that folks who wound up there would be mighty damned uncomfortable . . . so to speak.

He let out a groan that made the throbbing inside his skull even worse. Definitely alive, he thought.

Now he just had to take things one at a time. Open his eyes. Ignore the pain. Get his hands underneath him and push himself up. Slow and easy, Fargo warned himself. Slow and easy . . .

The only problem with that was a sense of urgency nagging at his brain, warning him that he needed to move quickly. He needed to be up on his feet, taking action. He just couldn't quite remember *why* he felt that way.

Then it hit him.

Elizabeth!

The memories came flooding back then: the gunshots from the trading post, the muzzle flashes in the darkness, the terrible blow on his head, Elizabeth's screams as she was dragged away. . . .

Fargo found himself on his feet with no clear knowledge of how he came to be standing. He lifted his right hand to his head and found a sore, sticky place in his hair above his ear. Even the gentlest touch set off an anvil chorus inside his skull.

The bullet that had struck him there had barely grazed him. The skin was hardly broken and the wound hadn't bled much. But it had been enough to knock him out. Fargo had no idea how long he had been unconscious. The night was quiet again. The shooting had stopped.

Fargo took a deep breath, but other than that, stood absolutely still, listening intently and letting the clamor in his head die down a little. He became aware of a faint crackling sound. As the wind shifted slightly, the smell of smoke came to his nostrils.

Alarmed, he stumbled over to the edge of the trees and looked down the hill toward the trading post. He saw what he was afraid he'd see. Flames leaped from the roof of the building, and smoke billowed up from it into the night sky.

Fargo swung around and gave an urgent whistle. The Ovaro answered with a shrill whinny. Fargo hurried toward the sound, and a moment later found the big black-and-white horse. He hung on to the stallion's neck for a moment to catch his breath and then swung up bareback onto the horse.

It was only after he had ridden hurriedly halfway down the hill that he realized he was unarmed.

Too late to do anything about that now, he told himself grimly. He had to get down there to the trading post, in case there was still anyone there who needed his help.

The fire was burning strongly when Fargo slid off the Ovaro in front of the building. "McAllister!" he shouted over the roaring and crackling of the flames.

A nightmarish glare spilled out the open front door of the building. "Andrew! Angus! Elizabeth!"

No one answered.

He looked around and spotted a dark shape sprawled on the porch at the corner of the building. Fargo reached the porch in a couple of bounds and ran toward the fallen man. As he did so, the fire reached the roof over the porch, and it began to burn as well. Glowing sparks rained down around Fargo, stinging his bare torso.

The man lying on the porch wasn't moving. Fargo reached him, dropped to a knee, and grabbed hold of his shoulders to roll him onto his back. He wasn't surprised to see the face of Angus McAllister. Fargo checked for a pulse in McAllister's throat and was relieved when he found one. It was rapid and a bit irregular, but fairly strong.

Something crashed behind Fargo. He looked over his shoulder to see that part of the burning porch roof had fallen in. He had to get McAllister away from here before the rest of it collapsed.

Ignoring his own pains, Fargo bent and got his arms around the unconscious trader. With a grunt of effort, he straightened and lurched toward the edge of the porch. He couldn't get back to the steps—there was too much flaming debris in the way.

Fargo lunged against the railing. It broke under the weight of his and McAllister's bodies, and the two men fell off the porch and sprawled on the ground. Fargo scrambled up, got hold of McAllister's legs, and dragged him away from the blazing building. He didn't stop until he had put a safe distance between them and the flames.

McAllister groaned as he began to come around. Fargo knelt beside him and helped him sit up.

"McAllister!" he said. "Can you hear me? Do you understand me?"

McAllister blinked bleary eyes. "F-Fargo?" he gasped out.

"That's right." Fargo ran his hand over McAllister's body and found a large splotch of blood on his side. He wasn't sure how badly the Scotsman was wounded, but finding out would have to wait. "Listen to me. Where's Andrew?"

"Andrew? I . . . I dinna ken. . . ."

"Is he in the trading post?" Fargo knew that time was fleeting. If Andrew McAllister was still inside the building, it might already be too late to save him.

"I . . . I dinna ken," McAllister said again. "I dinna see him . . . after th' shootin' started. . . ."

"Was it Olney's men?"

"Aye . . . they came up an' called to me . . . wanted me to come out on th' porch . . . an' when I did, they started shootin'. . . ."

The roof of the trading post collapsed, sending a huge pillar of sparks gushing high into the sky. Fargo looked over his shoulder at the devastation and knew that anyone who had still been inside the building was now dead. There was no hope of survival. The realization was a bitter, sour taste on his tongue—the taste of defeat.

That reaction lasted only a second, however, before Fargo's iron will threw it off. He didn't know that Andrew had been inside the trading post. Until he had proof to the contrary, he was going to hope that the youngster had escaped.

He turned back to McAllister and asked, "Have you seen Elizabeth?"

"Nay . . . no' since . . . after supper . . ."

Fargo was relatively certain that Elizabeth had been

carried off by the men who had shot him. They must have been preparing to attack the trading post when they spotted Elizabeth sneaking out. Some of the men had followed her, while the others remained behind to carry out their treacherous raid. Fargo didn't know exactly who was behind this violence, but he would have bet on the gunman called Prescott.

It made no sense, though. Why attack the trading post, shoot McAllister, and burn the place to the ground? McAllister hadn't done anything to those hardcases. What could he have had that they wanted?

He would have to figure that out later, Fargo told himself. Right now he had to tend to McAllister. He ripped the trader's shirt open, laying bare the wound in his side. By the light of the blazing trading post, Fargo examined the injury and saw that a bullet had plowed a fairly deep furrow in McAllister's side. It was difficult to tell because the wound had bled so much, but Fargo thought the slug probably had missed the vital organs. The injury was painful and messy, but with any luck, it wouldn't be life threatening.

The men who had gunned down McAllister must have thought he was hit harder than he really was, or else they would have put a few more slugs in him to finish him off. The same was true of Fargo's situation. The hardcases he had swapped lead with had gotten overconfident and thought that his head wound was fatal.

They would regret that before he was through with them, Fargo vowed silently. They would be sorry as hell.

He stood and looked along the river toward the spot where Olney's expedition had been camped. It came as no surprise when he saw that all the wagons were gone, along with the horses and mules. The whole lot of them had pulled out, even though it was night. Prescott and the others probably wanted to put some distance between themselves and the scene of this atrocity.

"Come on," he said to McAllister as he helped the wounded man to his feet. "Let's get you away from here. Can you get on my horse?"

"I'll . . . try," McAllister grated out.

Fargo wasn't in the greatest shape himself, but he was better off than McAllister. He struggled, and after a few minutes, got the trader on the Ovaro's back. McAllister slumped forward over the stallion's neck and clung to its mane. Fargo walked toward the former site of Olney's camp. The Ovaro followed, moving at an easy walk that wouldn't dislodge McAllister.

A wave of dizziness swept over Fargo. He paused and put a hand on the stallion's shoulder to steady himself. He had to keep moving, he told himself. He couldn't afford to give in to the punishment he had received. After a moment, he began to feel stronger and walked on toward the river.

Embers still glowed in the remains of the expedition's camp fire. The wagons hadn't been gone for too long. Fargo wondered what had happened to Olney and Victoria. Had Prescott and the others killed them? Or had they been taken prisoner like Elizabeth?

Olney and his sister came from a wealthy family, Fargo reminded himself. Maybe Prescott had decided to kidnap them and hold them for ransom, and had convinced the other men to go along with the plan. They could have gunned down McAllister and set fire to the trading post in order to eliminate witnesses who could tie them to the crime.

The theory didn't seem quite right, but he had other concerns at the moment. He helped McAllister dismount and then got the trader stretched out on the grassy bank of the river.

"You'll be all right here for a little while," Fargo told him. "That bunch won't be coming back. The rest of my gear isn't far off. I'll go get it, and when I get back, I'll patch up that bullet hole in your side."

"F-Fargo." McAllister clutched at the Trailsman's arm. "Ye'll be . . . goin' after those . . . sons o' bitches . . . won't ye?"

"You can count on that," Fargo told him grimly.

Straightening, Fargo turned back toward the Ovaro. But before he could ride back up to his camp on the hilltop, he was distracted by a sudden groan that came from somewhere nearby. Somebody else was here, and from the sound of it, they were hurt.

The man groaned again. Fargo followed the sound under the trees along the river. About twenty yards away, he practically stumbled over a recumbent form. He bent over and lifted the man's head out of the shadows into a stray beam of moonlight. He saw Jeb Tolbert's lean face, now partially covered with a smear of dark blood.

"Tolbert!" Fargo said. "What happened to you?"

"Sh-shot," Tolbert gasped out. "Somebody . . . walloped me. . . . Then Prescott . . . that bastard . . . shot me . . . to pieces."

Here was confirmation, as if Fargo had needed it, that Prescott was responsible for what had happened tonight. He quickly checked Tolbert's body, and found a wound in the mountain man's left thigh and a couple in his torso.

"Let me give you a hand," Fargo said. He got hold of Tolbert under the arms and lifted him. Tolbert gasped in pain when he tried to put weight on his wounded leg. He would have collapsed if Fargo hadn't been behind him, holding him up.

"Feels like . . . my leg's busted," he grated out. "Bullet must've . . . got the bone."

"You're probably right," Fargo said. "I'm going to take you over by the river. McAllister's there. He's wounded, too."

Tolbert tried to say something, but Fargo told him to take it easy. There would be time for talking later, once he had tended to the wounds of both men. He half-carried, half-dragged Tolbert over to the spot where he had left Angus McAllister. As carefully as possible, he lowered Tolbert to the ground beside McAllister.

When Fargo straightened, another wave of dizziness hit him. This time he wasn't close enough to the Ovaro to grab on to the horse and brace himself. He fell, unable to keep his balance, and the impact when he hit the ground sent more shocks of agony through him, especially inside his head.

He had a pretty thick skull, but it had taken too much punishment in the past few days, he realized. First Baird had clouted him with that broken branch, and now his head had been kissed by a bullet. Maybe his skull was fractured and he just didn't know it. Blinding pain filled his brain.

He tried to push himself up, but couldn't make it. As he slid down to the ground again, he thought about what Tolbert had said about there being wolf sign in the area. If there were wolves around and they came upon the three injured men lying beside the river, they would have themselves a feast. The Ovaro would stay close to Fargo and try to protect him. But even the big stallion wouldn't be able to run off a whole pack of wolves.

That thought made Fargo renew his efforts to get up, but again his muscles and his head betrayed him. He slumped down, unaware now that he was lying on the ground. It seemed to him more like he was afloat on a sea of pain.

When oblivion claimed him, it was a blessed relief.

*　　*　　*

He rose slowly out of nothingness. Wherever he was, it was still dark. Dark and cool . . . After a few minutes, Fargo realized there was a damp cloth draped over his face. It felt wonderful.

He must have stirred enough to draw attention to the fact that he was awake. A voice he recognized as Angus McAllister's said, "Rest easy, Fargo. Dinna try to move."

Fargo followed that advice. He remembered his head being filled with agony, and some instinct warned him that if he tried to move, the pain might come back.

The cloth was lifted from his eyes. He could see now, although there wasn't much to see except a flickering red glow off to one side. He felt heat on that side as well and knew he was lying beside a camp fire.

A dark shape loomed above him. McAllister . . . "Ye'll be all right," the trader told him. "Ye just need to rest that head o' yers. Ye took one too many hard knocks on it, I reckon."

Fargo thought that was probably right. He was surprised to see that McAllister was already up and around and able to build a fire. He tried to form words, but his tongue was dry and awkward. McAllister held a cup to his mouth, and Fargo took a couple of swallows of cold water. They tasted wonderful.

"H-how long . . . have I been out?" he rasped. "How many . . . hours?" He was thinking about Elizabeth. He had to get started after Prescott and the others, so that he could catch up to them before any harm had a chance to befall her.

"Hours?" repeated McAllister. " 'Tis sorry I be to tell ye this, Fargo, but ye been outta yer head for three days an' nights."

The news burst on Fargo with stunning force. He

closed his eyes and groaned. It seemed impossible that he had been unconscious for that long. And yet McAllister would have had no reason to lie about such a thing. Fargo had to accept that it was true.

"What about . . . Tolbert?" he asked.

"I'm here," the mountain man's voice answered from somewhere nearby. It sounded fairly strong, too. Fargo risked turning his head and saw Tolbert sitting a few feet away, with his back propped up against a log. He had a blanket around his shoulders, but Fargo could still see the bandages wrapped around his mid-section. There was one around his head, too. Tolbert's left leg was stretched out straight in front of him, splinted with branches that had been lashed tightly to it on each side.

McAllister had a bandage about his torso as well. He moved gingerly as he went around the fire to pour a cup of coffee. He brought the cup back to Fargo and got an arm under the Trailsman's shoulders so he could lift him to sip from the cup. Fargo recognized the cup and the coffeepot. They were from his gear.

The strong, bracing brew gave Fargo some strength. After a few sips, he was able to say, "Tell me . . . what happened."

"I reckon we all three laid there on th' riverbank all night, helpless as wee bairns," said McAllister. " 'Tis fortunate nothin' else happened to us. Th' good Lord was smilin' down on us from Heaven."

Tolbert took up the story. "Come mornin', Angus and me woke up. You were still out cold, Fargo. Angus was able to get up and crawl over to where I was."

"I'd lost some blood, so I was mighty weak," McAllister said. "And me side was stiff where that bullet hit me, but I could move around some."

Tolbert grunted. "A good thing, too, because he

was able to gather a little wood and get a fire started. Then he fetched some water from the river and tried to clean up my wounds."

"I didna expect th' poor fella to live, as many times as he was hit," McAllister said with a grim chuckle. "But Jeb surprised me. He's a stubborn old coot."

"I ain't the only one," Tolbert said pointedly. He turned back to Fargo and went on. "Anyway, Angus patched me up as best he could, and then when I felt a little better, I returned the favor for him. There didn't seem to be anything we could do for you, Fargo, except keep you warm. You've just got a little scratch on your head, but you were sure out cold."

"When a man gets hit on th' head by a bullet, 'tis a tricky thing," McAllister said.

Tolbert touched the bandage tied around his head. "Yeah, this gash on my skull came from a pistol barrel, so it ain't as bad. I ain't sure which one of the bastards it was who hit me, but it was Prescott who gunned me, I know that. Son of a bitch laughed when he did it, too."

Fargo wasn't surprised. He had known from the first time he saw Prescott that the man was dangerous, and maybe even mentally unstable.

"Anyway, Prescott busted my leg with a bullet and put a couple more slugs through me," Tolbert continued. "I reckon they must've missed everything important, though, because I'm still kickin'. Well, not kickin', exactly, not with a broken leg, but you know what I mean."

"Where's Stanton?" Fargo asked.

Tight lines creased Tolbert's face. "Dead," he said flatly. "Angus found his body, not far from where I got shot. They'd gunned him down, too, only they did a better job of it. I ain't surprised. I knew ol' Bart would never go along with what they wanted."

Fargo's curiosity got the best of his weakness. He pushed himself up on an elbow and asked, "What do you mean by that?"

"Takin' those two youngsters."

Fargo's gaze went to McAllister, who looked equally as grim as Tolbert. "Elizabeth and Andrew?" he asked in a hushed tone.

"Aye," McAllister replied. "Those scoundrels ha' taken both o' them. Jeb told me about it when he was strong enough."

"Locked 'em up in cages just like animals," Tolbert said, his voice shaking a little from the depth of his anger. "I know that's what they did with the boy, because I saw it with my own eyes. I reckon they did the same with the girl, too."

"Back up," Fargo said. "Start at the beginning. Why would Prescott want Andrew and Elizabeth?"

"Prescott?" Tolbert shook his head. "Prescott led the attack on the trading post and gunned me down, but it weren't his idea. He was just followin' Olney's orders."

"Olney!"

"That's right," Tolbert said with a nod. "He said havin' a couple of live Injuns in his museum and exhibition would make it . . . what did he call it? 'A perfect representation of the untamed West,' or some such shit."

Fargo let his head fall back and closed his eyes as the enormity of what he'd just heard soaked in. Olney had kidnapped Elizabeth and Andrew to take them back to Philadelphia and put them on display. How could anyone do such a thing?

Fargo opened his eyes again and said, "He can't get away with it. You're talking about a couple of human beings. The authorities won't let Olney keep them locked up in cages like that, against their will."

"I'm talkin' about Injuns," Tolbert said. "Mighty educated Injuns, maybe, but they're still redskins." He glanced at McAllister. "No offense, Angus. I'm just tellin' it the way folks back east will see it."

"I understand," McAllister said.

Fargo didn't, but he knew that Tolbert was probably right. Olney was rich. The law wasn't going to come after him just to free a couple of Indians.

"I think that sister of his had something to do with it, too," Tolbert went on. "She pure-dee hated Miss Elizabeth after the two of 'em got into that ruckus in the trading post. I wouldn't be surprised if she was the one who put the idea in Olney's head. Once he thought about it, though, he was all for it. Said he could study the two of them and it'd 'further the cause of natural science.' Bunch o' nonsense if you ask me, but that's what he said."

"And Prescott and the others went along with it," Fargo said.

"Sure. Olney was payin' 'em good money. And Prescott ain't the sort to draw the line at dirty work. Olney didn't approach me and Bart, though, until after all hell had already started poppin'. I reckon he knew we'd try to stop him if we could. By the time we knew what was goin' on, they'd already shot Angus and grabbed the boy. Some of them threw him in one o' the cages while the others set fire to the tradin' post. Olney told me what was goin' on and offered me a bonus if I'd go along with them. I told him to go to hell and tried to get to the boy and set him free. That's when somebody pistol-whipped me and then Prescott shot me."

"At least ye tried to help," McAllister said. "I'm thankin' ye for that, Jeb."

Fargo closed his eyes again while he thought about everything he had learned. Though he was surprised to hear that Richard Francis Olney and Victoria Arrowsmith were to blame for the violence that had broken out, the news didn't come as a complete shock. He had known that Victoria hated Elizabeth. Olney had the same sort of moral blind spot when it came to science that some men did. To him, nothing mattered except the exhibition he was going to put on back in Philadelphia.

McAllister went on. "I salvaged as much as I could from th' tradin' post and made this camp here for us. I found th' camp ye had made up on th' hill, too, and brung all yer outfit down here." He smiled solemnly. "Ye didna go very far when I told ye to leave, did ye, Skye?"

"I wanted to . . . keep an eye on things," Fargo murmured.

"An' 'tis a good thing that ye did. If ye hadna pulled me away from th' tradin' post, I'd ha' burned up along wi' it."

"And if Angus hadn't been around to take care o' me, I'd have probably died, too," Tolbert put in. "I reckon you saved us both, Fargo."

"But not Andrew and Elizabeth," Fargo said bitterly. He started to push himself up again. "I've got to go after them. If they've only got a three-day start, I can catch up to them. Those wagons can't move very fast—"

The dizziness hit him and forced him back down to the ground. He cursed in anger and frustration.

McAllister came to him and rested a hand on his shoulder. "Ye just woke up after bein' out cold for three days. I'm worried about th' lad an' the lassie, too, but ye canna just mount up an' gallop after them, th' shape yer in. Ye got to rest an' get yer strength back."

"Give it a day or two, Fargo," Tolbert urged. "You

141

know this country out here. Hell, you probably know it better than anybody. You could catch up to those wagons if they had a week's start on you." The mountain man laughed humorlessly. "I'd go with you, but I reckon with this busted leg, it'll be a long time before I'm up to a hard ride."

"And you need to stay here and take care of Jeb, Angus," Fargo muttered. "It's up to me."

"Aye," McAllister agreed. "But I ken th' sort o' man ye are, Skye Fargo, despite any harsh words I mighta had for ye." His hand closed tightly on Fargo's shoulder. "I know that if there's any man alive who can bring me children back safely to me . . . 'tis the Trailsman."

10

Another thirty-six hours passed with maddening slowness before Fargo was able to saddle the Ovaro and ride out. The first twelve of those hours, he had been unable to sit up without blinding pain filling his head. For the next twelve hours after that, he could sit up and eat and look around. But when he tried to get to his feet, he was too dizzy to stand. Finally, his head settled down to the point that he was able to get up and move around. His willpower and hardy constitution took over, and strength flowed back into his body. Even though he wasn't completely back to normal by the time he took up the trail, he felt good enough so that he knew he couldn't delay any longer.

He shook hands with McAllister and Tolbert before he rode out. "Take care o' yerself, Skye," McAllister urged. " 'Tis a mighty bad bunch ye'll be goin' up against."

"Angus is right," Tolbert agreed. "Prescott's kill crazy, and the others ain't much better. Any of 'em would shoot you in the back for a nickel."

Fargo nodded grimly. "I'll be back," he promised as he swung up into the saddle. His heels lightly touched the Ovaro's flanks, and the big stallion broke into a ground-eating lope.

Fargo rode east through the pass that had brought him to the Gallatin River Valley. Not far beyond it, he came to the Yellowstone River. From here on out, although there were ranges of hills in his path, the really rugged mountains were behind him. He could now make better time. But that had been true for the wagons, as well, once they made it through the pass.

The trail was easy to follow. Six large, heavy wagons and a coach, along with a dozen or so riders, left plenty of sign. It didn't take a miraculous tracker like old James Fenimore Cooper's Hawkeye to follow a trail like that.

Fargo wouldn't have minded having a couple of fierce Mohican warriors with him to sort of even up the odds, though.

Olney's party had had five days' start on him. Fargo pushed the Ovaro, knowing that the stallion had the strength and stamina to cut down that lead. He rode from before dawn to after dark every day, living on jerky that he gnawed while in the saddle, washed down with sips of water from his canteen. The only pauses during the day were short stops to let the Ovaro rest a little. Fargo knew that he was pushing himself, too. He couldn't afford to do otherwise.

The clean, high country air, the crisp temperatures, and the warm sun had all combined to have a great healing, revitalizing effect on him. But his head still hurt from time to time and he knew he needed more rest. There would be plenty of opportunities for that after he had rescued Elizabeth and Andrew, he told himself.

He had tried to figure out a strategy for accomplishing that goal, but it was futile until he caught up with the wagons. He wouldn't know what the situation was until he could see it for himself.

A week passed, and now the mountains were far behind him. He rode over rolling, thickly grassed hills. The plains stretched out in front of him, sweeping all the way to the valley of the Mississippi.

As the terrain grew more level, Fargo rode even harder. The Ovaro responded magnificently, as Fargo expected, but even the valiant stallion's strength wasn't endless. This long chase had to end soon.

On the eighth day, he caught sight of the wagons. They were still far in front of him, but at least he could see them now. That lifted his spirits considerably. He slowed down a little, not wanting to get too close while the sun was up.

Prescott was cunning enough that he probably had men keeping an eye on their back trail, even though he wouldn't be expecting any pursuit. As far as Prescott knew, everyone who had been left behind was dead.

He was in for a mighty big surprise, Fargo thought with a grim smile.

Fargo kept moving after dark, looking for a camp fire up ahead. When he didn't see one, he decided that the expedition must have made a cold camp, not wanting to attract the attention of any bands of Pawnee, Kiowa, or Sioux that might be wandering nearby on the plains.

Fargo slowed the Ovaro to a walk. He didn't want to ride right into the middle of the camp without realizing it. He was vastly outnumbered, and the element of surprise was just about the only thing he had on his side.

He was still racking his brain, trying to come up with some way to lessen the odds against him. He could pick off some of the hardcases at long range with the Henry, but only a few. Then the others would know he was after them. It would be better if he could strike quickly, with devastating effectiveness. . . .

He smelled the answer before he saw it. The odor was rank and penetrating and unmistakable to anyone who had spent much time out here on the plains. Fargo rode slowly up the long, gentle slope of a hill. When he topped it, he saw the small herd of buffalo spread out before him like a black pool in the moonlight.

There were only a few hundred of them, probably an offshoot from a much larger herd somewhere not far off. It was said that a man could sit on a hill and watch a single buffalo herd go by all day without ever coming to an end. Fargo knew that was true. He had seen herds that had to number in the millions, if not the tens of millions.

This bunch was the perfect size for his purposes, though. They were dozing right now, but come morning, they would be up and moving again, drifting slowly across the prairie as they grazed.

Fargo swung around the herd, giving it a wide berth so the buffalo wouldn't know he was there. He had to find the Olney expedition's camp and scout it out before he would know if his rudimentary plan had even a chance in hell of succeeding.

Some instinct warned him to dismount and advance on foot. A short time later, he heard voices. Leaving the Ovaro with the reins dangling, knowing the big horse wouldn't stray, Fargo crawled to the top of a small rise and peered down at the camp.

As he had suspected, there was no fire. The wagons had not been drawn in a circle, and the teams were still hitched in case they had to pull out in a hurry.

Prescott, or whoever was in charge of the practical details, was being cautious.

The coach was parked at the tail end of the little caravan, as usual, and a tent had been pitched beside it. That would be Olney's tent, Fargo thought. He recalled that Victoria spent her nights inside the coach. Fargo's keen eyes spotted a few men standing guard with rifles around the camp, but the others had spread their bedrolls next to the wagons. A coughing growl came faintly from one of the cages. That would be the mountain lion, probably pacing restlessly back and forth, no doubt still wondering what in the world had happened to it.

Fargo wondered which of the cages contained Elizabeth and Andrew McAllister. There was no way he could tell in the darkness, and he couldn't risk trying to sneak into the camp. If he hadn't been alone, he might have given it a try, but he knew that he was the only one within hundreds of miles who could help the two young prisoners. He had to try the plan that had occurred to him earlier, even though it was a desperate one and held dangers of its own.

He slipped back to the Ovaro and led the horse away from the camp. The buffalo herd was about a mile away. Fargo circled back around the shaggy beasts and finally stopped to spread his bedroll. A little before dawn would be the time to put his plan into action, he thought. He needed to be able to see, at least a little.

Until then, he fell into a light sleep, knowing that the built-in alarm in his brain would awaken him at the right time.

A chill hung over the plains when Fargo rose the next morning. The eastern sky was gray, but streaks of pink and orange began to appear along the horizon as he mounted up and rode toward the buffalo herd. The plains were largely without landmarks, but Fargo's instincts told him where the expedition's camp lay and where he needed to be as he approached the herd. When he crested a rise and saw the buffalo, the beasts were already up and grazing, moving ever so slowly toward the south.

That was the wrong direction. Fargo rode alongside the herd, about a hundred yards away, and took off his hat to wave it over his head. Even at this distance, he heard the snorts as some of the buffalo noticed him and took offense at his presence. He edged closer, still waving the hat in circles. The leaders of the herd veered away from him, and the others followed.

"That's it," Fargo said quietly. "That's the way, you big, shaggy varmints!"

He rode still closer, and the buffalo began to move faster. If the herd turned the wrong way and stampeded toward him, he and the Ovaro would have to race for their lives. But it was easier for the buffalo to try to get away from this puny, annoying human, so that was what they did. The sound of their hooves against the earth rose to a rumble as they moved faster and faster.

Suddenly, the leaders lurched into a run, and the hundreds of other animals in the herd followed suit. Fargo grinned and clapped his hat back on his head as the herd broke into a full-fledged stampede. Like a black-and-brown wave, the buffalo swept up over a rise and thundered on toward the east—right toward the spot where the Olney expedition was camped.

Fargo had pointed the herd toward the camp and fired it like a bullet from a gun. Never wavering, the buffalo pounded on and on. Now the sound of the stampede was an earthshaking roar rather than a rumble. Fargo galloped along behind them. He pulled his bandanna up over the lower half of his face to protect his mouth and nose from the choking clouds of dust that rose in the stampede's wake.

Up ahead in the camp, they must have heard the buffalo by now. Fargo could imagine the men rolling frantically out of their blankets and rushing around to get their horses saddled and the wagons ready to roll. They wouldn't have time, though. At rest, a buffalo was a placid, slow-moving creature. But once the herd was caught in the throes of a panic, they moved incredibly fast.

The Ovaro lunged up a slope and over the top, and in the soft light of dawn, Fargo saw the camp in front of him. Figures scurried desperately here and there as the buffalo herd closed in on them. There was too much dust in the air. Fargo couldn't tell exactly what was going on, and couldn't recognize any of the figures.

But he saw some of them go down as the shaggy tide reached them. The screams that must have gone up were drowned out by the thundering hooves.

If there had been more buffalo, Fargo wouldn't have tried this. Thousands of the animals would have packed together in a compact mass that would have slammed into the wagons, turned them over, and broken them open to trample anything inside.

As it was, though, the herd had spread out somewhat. Fargo saw that the buffalo were doing as he had hoped they would: swerving around the heavy wagons. The wagons were jolted back and forth as the buffalo brushed against them, but none of the vehicles tipped over and neither did the coach.

The horses and mules and the men who were caught in the open weren't as lucky. They were overrun, chopped into pieces by the hooves of the stampeding buffalo. Fargo's jaw tightened grimly as he thought about the death and destruction he had unleashed on this early morning.

But those men had killed Bart Stanton, done their best to kill him, Angus McAllister, and Jed Tolbert, and kidnapped Elizabeth and Andrew. Fargo wasn't going to lose much sleep over the fate that had thundered down on them out of the dawn.

It took only moments for the herd to sweep through the camp, leaving behind devastation. Fargo saw, as he rode closer, that one of the wagons had tipped over at last, but it hadn't been broken open. That was a stroke of luck.

He had his Colt in his hand, but he didn't know if anyone was left alive to put up a fight. As he rode in, that hope was shattered by the sudden blaze of gunfire. Colt flame bloomed in the shadows from under one of the wagons.

Some of the hardcases must have sought shelter there when the stampede hit. It would have been a hellish few minutes as the herd surged around them, the men expecting the wagon to tip over at any time, leaving them exposed to the stampede.

But that hadn't happened. Now, as they saw a lone rider following the buffalo into the camp, they had figured out what had happened and were taking out their anger on Fargo.

He went out of the saddle in a rolling dive as slugs sizzled around his head. He came up firing, triggering four shots toward the muzzle flashes under the wagon. He darted behind one of the other wagons to use it for cover. The pointed nose and banditlike eyes of a raccoon appeared at the opening between two of the slats. The little animal stared curiously at him.

No more shots came from the other wagon. Fargo reloaded the empty chambers in the Colt and edged carefully toward the spot where the gunmen had taken refuge. He spotted a couple of sprawled shapes on the ground. His bullets had brought them down.

Now he had to find Elizabeth and Andrew.

Suddenly, he heard Elizabeth screaming, "Skye! Skye! Over here!" Andrew joined in the shouting.

Fargo ran toward the wagon where they were caged. They had hold of the slats and were peering out through the gaps. Like all the other cages, the doors were on the top. Fargo would have to climb up to release them.

He holstered his gun as Elizabeth reached out between two of the slats. He took her hand and squeezed it. Tears ran down her cheeks as she pressed her face to the opening.

"Olney told us you were dead, Skye," she said. "I didn't want to believe it, but they said everybody back at the trading post was dead. Somehow, though, I knew you would come to help us."

"What about Pa?" Andrew asked from the cage next to his sister's. "What happened to him?"

"He's all right," Fargo reassured them. "He was wounded, but not too bad. I got him away from the trading post before it burned down."

"The trading post is gone?" Elizabeth asked in a choked voice.

"I'm afraid so. But it can be rebuilt." Fargo grinned. "Since all three of you McAllisters are still alive, I don't have any doubts that it will be."

He added that Jed Tolbert had survived the fighting, too, although with more serious injuries. Then he went to the back of the wagon, where rungs had been attached to form a ladder.

He had just started climbing when Elizabeth cried, "Skye, look out!" The words were barely out of her mouth when a shot blasted.

The bullet smacked into the wagon near Fargo's

151

face, chewing off splinters that stung his cheeks. With his left hand still grasping one of the rungs, he twisted his body and drew the Colt with his right hand. A second shot roared as he spotted the gunman. It was Prescott, crouched on top of one of the other wagons. He must have climbed up there and flattened out on the roof when the buffalo hit, Fargo thought. It had been a desperate gamble on the killer's part, but it had paid off. He had survived the stampede. And now he was doing his best to gun down the Trailsman.

Hanging on the makeshift ladder, Fargo jerked his revolver up and fired as he felt the wind-rip of Prescott's third shot beside his ear.

Fargo's bullet caught Prescott in the body and straightened him out of his crouch. He took a stumbling step backward and tried to bring up his gun for another shot.

Before Prescott could pull the trigger, though, there was a sharp cracking sound and he plunged out of sight. When Fargo heard the high-pitched howl of a mountain lion and the screams that came from inside the wagon, he knew what had happened.

The latch on the door atop the mountain lion's cage had broken under Prescott's weight. The door had fallen out from under the gunman, dropping him right on top of the enraged catamount. As Prescott's screams died away in a hideous gurgle, Fargo knew there was no point in checking on him. The mountain lion had finished him off.

Fargo holstered the Colt again and resumed his climb. When he reached the top, he unlatched the doors of the two cages. Then he extended an arm down to Elizabeth and Andrew in turn, hauling them up and out of their captivity. Elizabeth hugged him tightly as they knelt on top of the wagon. Fargo held her shivering form against him and stroked her hair.

As he did so, he grinned at Andrew and said, "I reckon you'd better reconsider the idea of hunting buffalo, Andrew. If not for the hand that herd gave me, you'd still be locked up."

"I know," the youngster said. "I guess I can find my heritage some other way."

Fargo nodded in agreement, then helped both of them climb down to the ground. Elizabeth averted her eyes from the grisly remains of the trampled hardcases. "Did any of them survive?" she asked.

"I don't know," Fargo replied. "One or two might have got on their horses and ridden out of the way of the stampede in time. If they did, I don't reckon they'll be coming back this way any time soon. I don't think we have anything to worry about from them."

"What about Olney, and that awful sister of his?"

"We're about to find out," Fargo said. "You two stay back."

With that, he walked toward the coach. His hand rested on the butt of his gun. If either of the siblings was still alive, he didn't trust them.

When he reached the coach, he grasped the handle on the door and jerked it open, then stepped back quickly. "All right, come on out," he said sharply. "Don't try anything."

Somewhat to his surprise, Richard Francis Olney was the first one to step out of the coach. The man looked pale and shaken, as well he might after having almost been caught in a buffalo stampede. He had either been inside the coach or had scrambled into it in time to escape.

"Don't shoot!" he pleaded as he lifted his hands. "Please don't kill me!"

"I ought to," Fargo growled. "Bart Stanton was a good man, and he's dead because of you." He jerked his head toward what was left of the hired hardcases.

"So are quite a few other men, even if they weren't as good as Stanton."

"I . . . I just wanted to further the cause of science—" Olney began.

The look in Fargo's eyes silenced him. "I don't believe in gunning down anybody in cold blood, not even a worthless polecat like you," Fargo said. "Don't make me change my mind."

"I'm sorry," Olney said miserably. "I'm so sorry."

"You should be. Where's your sister?"

"She's inside the coach." Olney turned his head. "You'd better come out, Victoria."

The woman stepped out of the coach, clutching a dressing gown tightly around her. "Skye!" she exclaimed when she saw Fargo. "Thank God! I prayed someone would come to rescue me. Richard went mad! He kidnapped those poor children, and he was holding me prisoner, too!"

Elizabeth stepped up beside Fargo and said coldly, "Don't believe her, Skye. She's lying. She was the one who suggested to her brother that he take us back to Philadelphia. She certainly gloated over it enough during the past few days."

Victoria's face turned hard as she realized she wasn't going to be able to lie her way out of this. "You redskinned slut!" she hissed. "You wanted to see civilization. Well, you would have gotten to see it, and civilization would have gotten to see what an Indian whore looks like!"

Elizabeth lunged forward, and Fargo didn't try to stop her. The young woman's fist shot out. The punch landed solidly on Victoria's jaw and sent her flying backward to crash into the side of the coach. Her dressing gown fell open, revealing a lot of creamy white flesh that didn't interest Fargo in the slightest

154

anymore. He'd had his fill of Mrs. Victoria Arrow-smith.

Victoria fell to her knees. Olney knelt beside her and put an arm around her shoulders. She began to sob as he held her shuddering form against him.

"What are you going to do with us?" Olney asked nervously as he looked up at Fargo's stern, forbidding countenance.

The expression on Fargo's face didn't soften a bit. His voice was as hard as flint as he rested his hand on his gun butt once again and said, "Now, that's a mighty interesting question."

"Do you think the two of them will ever make it back home?" Elizabeth asked as she and Fargo and Andrew rode toward the distant mountains. Behind them were the wagons with their now-empty cages. Fargo had released all the animals that had been captured by the expedition.

"I don't know," Fargo answered honestly as he shook his head. "I told them to follow the Yellowstone until it runs into the Missouri River. There's lots of traffic on the Big Muddy this time of year and quite a few riverboats will be coming along there. They ought to be able to flag one down from the shore within a few days of getting there. At least, they have a chance to make it. To my way of thinking, that's as much as they deserve. More than they deserve, maybe."

Several of the mules and horses had survived the buffalo stampede. Fargo had taken a couple of them for Elizabeth and Andrew to ride. Then he hitched the others to the coach. Olney and Victoria had some supplies. In addition, Fargo had scavenged a couple of rifles and some ammunition from the devastation and had taken them a mile east of the spot where the camp had stood. He left the rifles and ammunition there for Olney and Victoria to pick up as they passed by.

So they had the coach and a team to pull it; they had provisions; and they had the means to protect themselves and to hunt game if they needed to. A lot of people had crossed the plains with less.

Of course, those people had also had courage and determination. Fargo wasn't sure how much of those commodities Olney and Victoria possessed.

Still, their survival was in their own hands now. With luck, they would make it back to civilization. And along the way, Olney would have a chance to study the West at close range, and Victoria would have adventure aplenty. After all the harm they had caused, Fargo figured they were getting off pretty damned light.

"I still want to visit the East someday," Elizabeth said.

"There's nothing stopping you," Fargo told her. With his eyes on the mountains ahead of them, he went on. "That's the good thing about this country. . . . If you want something bad enough, it's there for you if you have the strength and determination to reach out and grab it. There's always hope."

And for the Trailsman, there would always be the majestic mountains and the big, arching sky, and the faint but undeniable call of distant trails, of places he had never seen.

Fargo would make sure that he got Elizabeth and Andrew safely back to their father. Then, as always, he would answer that call.

LOOKING FORWARD!
The following is the opening
section from the next novel in the exciting
Trailsman **series from Signet:**

THE TRAILSMAN #291

THE CUTTING KIND

Fort Laramie, 1860—there's a killer on the
loose along the Oregon Trail, and it looks
like no one but Skye Fargo can stop him.

Jess Van Cleef had killed three men in Independence,
Missouri, and then lit out for the West, somewhere
along the Oregon Trail. Nobody knew just where, exactly, he was heading, as he'd been in too much of a
hurry to tell them.

It wasn't so much that he'd killed the men that
made people take notice of what he'd done, though.
It was the *way* that he'd killed them.

"Skint 'em, is what he did," John Keller told Skye
Fargo. "Not entirely, the way you might think—just
the faces. Cut their faces right off 'em, the son of a

bitch. And then he carved on their chests and arms a little. You know he musta enjoyed it. Nobody does somethin' like that 'less he enjoys it."

Keller was taking it hard, Fargo thought, which was only natural. One of the men Van Cleef had killed was Keller's younger brother.

"Little Sammy never hurt a fly, by God," Keller said. "Sweet and innocent as a child, little Sammy was. Yet Van Cleef showed him no mercy."

The younger Keller's body had been found in an alley behind a whorehouse, and judging from what Fargo had heard from others, Van Cleef and Sammy had gotten into an argument over a soiled dove named Big Nose Rose. They'd left the whorehouse without settling anything because the madam, known as Flower of the West, or just Flower to her friends, of whom there were reputed to be many, had threatened them with the two-shoot gun she kept under the bar.

Nobody knew for sure what had happened after that, but most everybody was morally certain that Van Cleef had thrashed Sammy half to death in the alley, then stolen his face and done a little carving on him before running a knife blade between his ribs to finish him.

"I'd like to think he kilt him first," John Keller told Fargo, "but it just ain't in the cards. A man like Van Cleef don't do things that way. He likes hearin' the moanin' and cryin'. Not that Sammy woulda cried. He was a young 'un, but he was too tough for that."

Fargo nodded his agreement, though he'd never met Sammy. He and John Keller had met a couple of days ago and had shared a drink or two since then because they were more or less in the same profession. Keller was a guide who took trainfuls of pilgrims out on the

Oregon Trail, and Fargo was known as the Trailsman because of his ability to get from one place to another throughout the West. He'd led his share of wagon trains, mapped the land for stage lines, and done a hundred other like things to earn his keep.

Keller was about forty years old, with a seamed face and lank hair that hung down from beneath his battered felt hat. He hadn't taken a bath for a while, and there was dirt in the creases on his cheeks.

At the moment, both Keller and Fargo were unemployed. The reason in Fargo's case was that it was too far gone in the year for anyone to go much farther west along the Oregon Trail. The first snow had already fallen, and it would take a much more foolhardy man than Skye Fargo to try to push on to Oregon with a bunch of soft pilgrims in his charge. He'd brought one last small group as far as Fort Laramie, where they planned to winter before moving out again in the springtime.

Fargo would be long gone by then, as he had no interest in staying in one place for more than a short time, not if he could help it. He was a man for whom being on the move was a necessity of life, and he'd be leaving Fort Laramie soon, heading back east to see if there was some kind of job he could pick up.

John Keller's reason for lacking employment was of a different nature. He was riding the vengeance trail, looking for Jess Van Cleef, and his search had led him to Fort Laramie.

"I don't know as he's around here," Keller said, "but I heard he'd been seen out this way. Thinks the law can't reach him out here, and I guess he's right about that. But I can, by God, and I intend to. A man like him ought not be allowed to run free, and not just because of what he done to little Sammy. He's done it to others, and he'll do it to more if he gets the chance."

Fargo nodded again. He'd found that was all he needed to do to keep a conversation going with Keller, who was more than ready to do enough talking for the both of them.

They were in the Red Dog Saloon, which was, or wasn't, part of Fort Laramie, depending on your point of view.

Unlike a lot of forts, Laramie wasn't enclosed by a stockade or wall, though Fargo had heard that had been the original plan. Because of a shortage of money, or some other reason, the wall had never been built, and Laramie had become an open fort, more like a small town, depending on the troops garrisoned there for its protection.

And anywhere there was a fort, open or not, especially one on a trail that saw so many passing wagon trains full of thirsty easterners looking for a new home out west, a saloon or two was bound to prosper. The Red Dog was one of them.

It wasn't on the grounds of the fort itself. The soldiers, for the most part, took their drinks in the Soldier's Board. But the Red Dog was located close enough to the grounds to be within the fort's protection. It was frequented by traders, trappers, travelers, renegades, rascals, cardsharpers, and anyone else who happened to be in the vicinity and had a craving for liquor—and who wasn't too particular about its quality.

It was a little after noon, and the Red Dog was quiet. There was a broken down upright piano up against one wall, but no one was playing it. In the two days he'd been in Laramie, Fargo hadn't heard a single note come from it. Whether it was broken or whether there was no one who could play, Fargo neither knew nor cared.

In a corner of the saloon, a drunk was slumped across a table, snoring and occasionally scratching himself in his sleep. Four men gambled with cards, but without any notable enthusiasm, a few tables away from where Fargo and Keller sat talking. The bartender was leaning on his elbows, staring out across the chilly room as if he were somewhere warmer and cheerier, maybe down around Galveston, Texas, where the Gulf waves would be washing up on the beach. Fargo didn't much blame him.

"I'll get the son of a bitch Van Cleef," Keller said. "I know for sure I will."

Fargo nodded again, but he didn't really think Keller had much of a chance to find Van Cleef. A man could lose himself in the West without any trouble at all if that's what he wanted to do. Keller might know the country, but that didn't mean he could find Jess Van Cleef, not if Van Cleef didn't want to be found.

Two men came into the saloon, and Fargo's lake blue eyes narrowed at the sight of the blowing snow through the open door. The bigger of the two men pushed the door closed, but not before the blast of air they let inside had increased the room's chill.

The men stood looking around. One stood well over six feet tall, while the other was at least a foot shorter. Both wore beaver hats and buffalo robes against the cold, and both had thick salt-and-pepper beards that obscured their faces. Each carried an old Hawken rifle that had cost between twenty-five and thirty dollars when new, considerably more than any other rifle. They were fine weapons, but Fargo preferred his Henry.

The men brushed snow off their heavy robes and looked around the room. The tall one said, "Which one of you fellas is John Keller?"

His voice was high-pitched and rusty, as if he didn't use it often.

Fargo looked at Keller to see if he'd respond. Keller looked down at his drink glass, which was almost empty.

"We want to hire John Keller for a guide," the short man said. "Pay's good."

His voice was a deep, rumbling bass. Fargo could have sworn that it vibrated through the floorboards of the saloon.

Keller looked up when the word *pay* was mentioned.

"I'm Keller," he said, turning to look at the two men. "What can I do for you?"

The two men eyed him silently, then looked at each other. After the silence had stretched for a while, the tall one said, "He don't look like much."

"Don't matter," his companion said. "He's the one we want."

"Want for what?" Keller said.

The two men looked at each other again, then turned back to Keller.

"To help me kill a man," the short one said.

The big man's name was Tobias Walker, and his shorter friend was Seth Gant.

The man they wanted to kill was Jess Van Cleef.

So naturally Keller was interested to hear what they had to say.

Fargo wasn't, not particularly, but he didn't see the need to get up and leave. It was a lot colder outside than it was in the saloon.

"Army won't do nothing about Van Cleef," Walker said, his voice not sounding so rusty after having been lubricated with a drink or two of the Red Dog's bad whiskey. "They say it ain't their job."

"They say they're here to protect people from the Injuns, not from some fella that might be back in Independence by now," Gant said, his voice vibrating the table where they sat.

"Somebody's gotta do something, though," Walker said, "and we hear you'd like to."

He was talking to Keller, of course. Both men had pretty much ignored Fargo ever since sitting down.

Their story was simple. They had once been trappers and hunters before leaving the mountains and going back east to find wives.

"Made a pile of money out of those mountains," Walker said, "but it gets mighty lonesome up there after a while. Not a whole lot of women around. Some folks ain't bothered by that, but me and Gant are. So we decided to try the civilized life for a while."

His lip didn't quite curl when he said "civilized," but they came close.

Gant's did. "*Civilized*, my ass. A city is a sinkhole of corruption. We should've brought our wives back out here and lived in the mountains. Both of 'em would still be alive now, instead of just yours."

Gant's wife was the one Van Cleef had killed. It seemed that as he was leaving Independence, he stopped off at Gant's house, maybe because he wanted to steal something, or maybe just because he thought he could find a little entertainment before beginning his long trip west.

What he'd found was Gant's wife, who was in the kitchen, baking bread. Van Cleef raped her and killed her, then cut her up. Badly.

"Wasn't much left of her face," Walker said. "The bastard was blood crazy. Neighbor woman happened by just as he was leaving, and he raped her, too. Didn't kill her outright, and that was his mistake. She was able to tell what happened to her before she died."

Keller nodded with understanding. He said, "I know about Van Cleef, all right, and I'd like to see him dead. What I don't know is why you two don't just find him and kill him yourselves. You look like you know this country as well as I do. Maybe better."

"Ain't a matter of knowing the country," Gant said.

He looked at Walker, who looked down at his drink as if it had suddenly become the most interesting thing in the room.

"It's a matter of a man who's pussy-whipped," Gant continued.

"It ain't that," Walker said.

"If it ain't, what would you call it, then?"

Walker didn't say anything.

"Cat got your tongue?" Gant said.

Walker remained silent.

"His wife," Keller said. "She don't like the idea of him going out after Van Cleef. Am I right?"

Gant nodded. "She said he could come as far as Laramie. If we hadn't found Van Cleef by then, he'd better get back to his little house and yard."

"And my son," Walker said. "Don't forget Benjamin."

"I ain't forgot him," Gant said, not sounding too happy about admitting it.

"You can't blame a man for wanting to be with his wife and son," Walker said, shaking his head. "You just can't."

Fargo had known plenty of men who wanted nothing more than a house, a wife, and a son, but he'd never had the urge to settle down himself. There was too much to do and see for a man to let himself be tied down like that.

"If we'd found Van Cleef before we got this far," Walker said, "I'd have killed him for you with my bare hands. But I promised Ruth I'd come back if we got to Laramie, and I got to keep that promise."

Fargo could understand promises, all right. They weren't to be made lightly, and if you made one, you kept it. At least Fargo did.

"And I can't go after the bastard by myself," Gant said. "But I got to go after him some way or other." He looked at Walker. "My wife ain't waitin' for me, thanks to that bastard Van Cleef. If I was twenty years younger, or even ten, I'd do the job on my own, but I'm just too damned old to go it alone."

He looked to Fargo to be a bit over sixty, older than Walker, who was no youngster himself.

"I reckon I'll go with you, then," Keller said. "You mentioned something about pay?"

He'd have gone for nothing, Fargo thought, but there wasn't anything wrong with making a little money to do something you wanted to do anyway.

Gant and Keller talked about the payment while Walker drank in silence and Fargo looked around the saloon. Nothing had changed. The drunk was still snoring, the card game continued, and the bartender still looked like he wished he were somewhere a long way off.

The discussion of money concluded, and Keller tapped a finger on the table and looked at Fargo.

"You want to go with us?" he said. "I'll split the money with you. Half for me, half for you."

The money was tempting, but Fargo didn't think they had much of a chance to catch Van Cleef. He said, "I'll be heading back east soon. I wish you luck."

"I could use some company," Walker said. "If you're of a mind to go Independence way."

"When are you leaving?"

Walker looked at Gant, who stared back without speaking. Walker gave his head a slight shake and turned back to Fargo.

"I guess I'll be leaving in the morning. Nothing to hold me here, not now that Seth's hooked up with Keller."

"I guess I'll go along, then," Fargo said.